THE PATTERNMAKER
AND THE TIDE

NEIL MACH

TO
HEIDI

HAVE A WONDERFUL
READ + THANKS
FOR YOUR SUPPORT

J Mac

The Patternmaker and the Tide

Neil Mach

© Copyright June 2022

The right of Neil Mach to be identified as author of this work has been asserted by him in accordance with the Copyright, Designs and Patents Act 1988.

All Rights Reserved

No reproduction, copy or transmission of this publication may be made without written permission. No paragraph of this publication may be reproduced, copied, or transmitted save with the written permission of the publisher, or in accordance with the provisions of the Copyright Act 1956 (as amended.)

Any person who does any unauthorised act in relation to this publication may be liable to criminal prosecution and civil claims for damage.

A CIP catalogue record for this title is available from the British Library.

This is a work of fiction. Names, characters, businesses, places, events, and incidents are either the products of the author's imagination or used in a fictitious manner. Any resemblance to actual persons, living or dead, or actual events is purely coincidental

First Published in 2022

Cover Artwork by Andrea Orlic (Artrocity)

This eBook is licensed for your personal enjoyment only. This eBook may not be re-sold or given away to other people. If you would like to share this book with another person, please purchase an additional copy for each recipient. If you're reading this book and you did not purchase it, please purchase your own copy. Thank you for respecting the hard work of this author.

http://www.neilmach.me

❀ Created with Vellum

'The tide is high but I'm holding on...'
— John Holt & the Paragons

1

She perches her sodden underside on a flaked windowsill, and she observes. She does this *every* morning. Today is unusual. Why? She shakes her head.

A flutter at the very margin of her midriff extends through her bones. She rejects the troubling sensation as nothing more than profound *sleepiness*. Ignoring the bubbles in her stomach, she stares beyond flaws in the dreary curtain, to sniff mildew and corruption. She tugs away a stained hem to improve her view. Outside, a drizzle becomes a downpour. She scrutinises the mucky rain-droplets that bend and scoot across the glass. One blob behaves like an ant — scampering with a mind of its own — it scutters aimlessly. Is anything truly random? Or are all things predictable? She glances at the spirals in the lemon curd wallpaper: the paper has a mathematical design. Does nature follow arrangements of pattern? What about bubbles? What about foam? What about waves?

She attempts to wipe the water-ant away with her cuff. The blighter is on the other side of the pane. He is not real. The insect is only temporary. It does not even *exist* in her dimension. She gawks beyond the buggish trail, to see into the street. The rain slants across her view like heavy sheets, tarps of water battering onto an oily blacktop. She reckons she was lucky to get home without a *thorough* drenching. Yet, even so, her nylons are sopping. Yes, unmistakably tacky.

The rain hurtles along the road, rushing in from the burial ground on the corner. She has never witnessed rain coming from *such* an acute angle *ever* before. It typically arrives from the *other* side. Usually, it dashes inland from beach to church. The English describe this sort of rain *pissing*. Today it is *pissing* sideways!

She smiles — because *he* arrives. *He* is the reason she sits at her window every morning. The old man who lives opposite is fascinating. She's drawn by his logical reliability and meticulous precision. He's a retired soldier, she presumes. Probably a sergeant-major in a defunct regiment. He boasts a military bearing, even though he's long since retired. He is solid as a broom, buckram shouldered, swollen chested — with one hand held to his lower back, the other rigid by his side. Stiff and severe. Puffed and important. The old man has the look of self-satisfaction on his face.

Checking the pendant-watch on her tunic, she confirms the old man is on time — six thirty. *As always.*

Conceding her nylons are too squishy to tolerate a moment longer, she rolls them down her limbs, clear of her calves, to rest against her ankles.

The old man exercises for ten minutes on the porch. She knows this because she studies his habits. He does this *every* morning. His movements are utterly regularized. The old man will keep a record of his reps in a notebook. After that, he will nip inside, on squat little legs, to eat a nutritious breakfast. Bran and kippers, she supposes. The sort of breakfast a pensioned soldier will fix himself. At seven thirty-five the old man will blast out for a stroll to the beach, his scarf twisted around his starched collar, a modest cap flattened onto those white curls. And, on the harshest winter days, his sturdiest greatcoat will be pulled tight around his scrawny shoulders. Punctilious as always. She didn't know how long he walked each day. But she knew he'd be back by lunchtime. She always got out of bed just after noon. That's when she would check him anew.

Sensing her tummy complain, she tells it to *shush*, 'Wait till later. You will have cup-a-soup at three.'

The old man exercises every day regardless of what happens. He completes his movements on his red-brick porch. Every morning she studies his movements from her window. First, he takes six deep breaths, next he performs ten shoulder rolls. She counts them *with him*. After, he marches on the spot, tick-tock, *tick-tock*. No wonder the neighbours describe him as an automated machine. His arms sway soberly, his hands slap ancient thighs. It's as if is he's filled with dynamic potential. Next, the old-man completes ten pendulum bobs, arms held stiff like batons. Knee-lifts and self-regulated stretches follow.

At *that* point, the old man *usually* begins swimming motions. But today he does *not*. That's strange! He ceases his exercises.Why? It seems he is discomposed by a *blur* that he sees in the distance. The blur is a darkened smear and seems to be emerging from the end of the lane. The blur approaches fast. She sees the blur *too*. It's a dim outline of *something* that is not, at first glance, anywise, recognisable as *anything*. But then she understands what the hurtling blur must be... it *must be* the newspaper delivery boy. He's racing his bicycle. And heading for calamity.

The stupid boy rides pell-mell, no hands, from the graveyard end of the lane. He rides upright and carefree. The gale pushes him fast, so he coasts free-style. He has a nincompoop's expression on an idiotic, pock-marked, face. She thinks he resembles a grinning chimp.

A slippery drain cover and an unexpected gust of wind catch him out. She watches the spectacle unfold. A sudden swerve hauls him. The boy gets a slim grip on his handlebars — but it's too late. He veers, then he crashes. He comes to a halt with bone-crushing abruptness. Headlong into a concrete lamppost! The cycle slides along the road under its own momentum. It comes to rest five yards from the boy's body. But he lays crushed on the unyielding surface. His body is immediately outside the old-man's house.

~

Tipping from her window ledge to stand upright, she draws back the curtain to see what happens next. The old man hurries from his porch. He moves hastily to the aid of stricken youth. The old man stoops. He leans over the lad's crunched body.

She registers she must do *something* — passive scrutiny is not an option. She hesitates, then she pushes herself from the pane and scans her bedsit room. When she arrived home, earlier, she dropped her keys. But where? She pinpoints a glint on the mattress, so heads in that direction, only to sprawl *arse-over-tit* on the ragged linoleum. Those squelchy tights had tripped her! She forgot she rolled them to her ankles. She rips the things away, with the fury of a lion tamarin wrenching apart fruit, then she collects her keys. She tussles herself to the exit. She stuffs puny fingers into the sides of sodden ballet shoes, then drags the shoes onto clammy feet. She dashes for the stairs. She heads for the street.

Almost immediately she regrets she did not think to put on her pink jacket. She left it hooked by the door. The brutal squall gnaws at her naked arms and cruel raindrops nip into her neckline. She scurries across the glistening road to the scene of the mishap. She arrives in a fluttering state of confusion. She stoops beside the elderly man, a man she barely knows, a man she studies every morning from her window, and the man glances from the boy's body and studies her with worn, grey, eyes: 'Broken breastbone. Call 999. Get *yambulance*,' he says. He employs a peculiar West Country accent.

She looks at the boy's twisted body on the tarmac. Then she considers the old man. Now she knows why Mrs Slaviaro — her landlady — calls him the *mechanical tin-plate toy-soldier*. He is *much* smaller than he seems from her window. Down here, on the street, he is stunted. She guesses he only comes up to her shoulders.

She stands absentmindedly, like a giraffe distracted by an inaccessible leaf, then she jostles the youngfella's bicycle from the centre of the road, to pitch it somewhere near the old man's garden wall. This is so it won't get banged by traffic. She notices the front wheel is ruined.

'And grab a bolster...' the old man shouts, 'From indoors. To support his cracked crown. Door s'open.'

She feels lost. She doesn't know *how* to behave. *Where is her phone?* She remembers she left it on her bed.

'Use my phone in the hallway — dial 999,' he shouts.

She forces her gaze from the injured lad to the old-man's front door. The mechanical tin-plate toy-soldier ignores what she does next because he's busy cradling the boy's head. He clasps the skull with delicate, soft-cupped hands. She thinks the old man is about so say something tender, perhaps a prayer, to the boy. Maybe the boy is dead. But the lad moans. So he's not *gone*. Not yet *anyhow*.

So she footsteps up the neat, red-stone path to the old-man's front porch and finds it takes more effort than she might have expected. Her legs turn to goo, her ballet-pumps slide on the tiles, and her head feels wonky. Somehow, she arrives at the old man's threshold. She grins at this minor achievement. Then abruptly she's *inside* the old soldier's house. It smells of wax and camphor. Right away, she sees a primitive telephone positioned, superciliously, on a lacquered table. She picks up the receiver and hears a *purr*. She places her finger in hole number 9 and rotates the dial clockwise until it reaches the stop. She releases and repeats this action twice more. As luck would have it, she had used an ancient-type telephone like this *before* — in fact, it's the exact same phone most folks have in the old country.

'Emergency? Which service do you require?'

'Ambulance.' She almost said *yambulance*.

'Please wait — you will be placed in a queue and transferred to the next available call taker.'

She hears a series of clicks before a foreign-sounding voice comes to the line, 'Hello?'

'I need an ambulance quick,' she says, 'The paperboy has crashed. He is in shock, I think. And—'

'I require some details. What is your full name?'

'Eimear. Eimear Lambe.'

'I cannot understand what you are saying. Is anyone there who speaks English?'

'I speak English. I said my name is Eimear Lambe.'

'Please spell.'

'L-A-M-B-E — please hurry...'

'Spell your other name...'

'E-I-M-E-A-R'

'And your home address?'

'Er? This happened in the street. I am using another person's phone...'

'Is that person with you? Do they speak English? Please put an English-speaking person on the line.'

'There is nobody else here right now. The *other person* is doing something important right now. I speak perfectly good English. Can't you hear me? Is this a poor line?'

'What is your home address?'

'I am trying to explain about that... this accident happened in Spring Lane, outside number 137.'

'What is your telephone number?'

'What? You want this one?' She considers the dial on the antique machine. 'Or do you want my mobile? Only, I haven't got my mobile with me right now, because you see..'

'What is the nature of your emergency?'

'Like I said, the paperboy fell off his bike. He crashed into a lamppost...'

'How many people are injured?'

'Just one. The paperboy. Look, how long will this take? When will the ambulance get here?'

There is no reply. Just tapping sounds. Then the voice says, 'Taking notes...'

'Right.'

'Miss Lame?' The voice mispronounces her name. She shrugs. 'What is the full name and date of birth of the injured party?'

'How should I know? He is about sixteen, I suppose...'

'We need the exact details of the injured party. You must get them for me. I require those details to complete this report. Will you go fetch them for me? I will wait.'

'How can I do that? The boy is unconscious...'

'What relationship do you have with the injured person?'

'What?'

'I'm trying to establish your relationship with the injured party. We need full details for a report.'

'He's a stranger to me. Look, what is all this? Why are there so many questions? I saw an accident, and went to help...'

'What is your date of birth?'

'Uh-oh, I'm out of here...' She smashes the handset into the plastic cradle. *Bastards!* Why is everyone so awkward in this bloody country?

She wants to go out again, to help the old-man. But remembers he mumbled something about collecting a thing called a Bol Stir. *Con-cen-trate,* she tells herself. Breathe and try to *con-cen-trate.* Think. What the heck is a Bol Stir? She recognises she's shivering. *God, it's cold in this house. Don't they have any heating?*

She rumbles deeper into the unfamiliar home, to push open a few doors. She enters a pleasant room and scans around. There are two large seats: one fitted with an elegant cushion. She thinks about grabbing the cushion but notices it's richly embroidered. It will get ruined in the pissing rain. She looks around for something different. Something that might serve as a Bol Stir. She sees lots of display boxes perched on shelves or tucked into alcoves. They are made from wood. Rectangular containers, fitted with Perspex front windows. All with little models inside. She decides they are not suitable as Bol Stirs.

She goes to the kitchen. It's at the back of the house. It smells of turpentine. There's a pine table and two spindly chairs on the cracked linoleum. Both chairs have yellow pads attached to their bum-seats. She grabs the closest pad, but it doesn't come away when she tugs. She discovers it's fastened with white tape. She groans and curses, and she bends to unfasten the ribbons with fingers made of out of wriggle-worms that refuse to behave properly. In due course, though, she unfixes the damn thing. She pushes the soft yellow pad to her chest and races out of the house, back into the street. To help the old man.

Miracle of miracles, an ambulance has arrived. The ambulance-man crouches with the old man. Another attendant gets a stretcher-thing from the back of the van.

She goes to the old man with the yellow pad. He looks at the pad and he gives a bewildered expression. She guesses he doesn't need it anymore. The old man stands, 'Thank you. I will go to hospital.' He points to the *yambulance*.

She holds the cushion over her tummy for comfort. She does *not* know what to do next.

'Could you please pull my front door? Also, drop back my bolster,' the old man points to the yellow pad. He nods toward his house.

She gestures with a thumbs-up sign. *Do you need any more help?* But everyone is too busy to hear her thoughts. The old man and the technician get the broken-boy into the *yambulance*. She hears a tele-phone ringing from inside the old man's property. She's aware the paperboy is making louder grunting noises, which, she supposes, is a good sign. The traffic builds. The ambulance-man tidies things away, and he says *excuse me dear,* because she's getting in his way.

Eimear goes back to the old guy's house and stands by the door. She rests his yellow kitchen-cushion thingy against his wall. Since the emergency is over, she doesn't have the right to wander into his home, does she?

The telephone stops ringing. She pulls the front-door shut and hears a satisfactory *click*. She steps along the red tile path, her ballet shoes yelping and squealing. She sees the ambulance pull away.

The wind howls down the street.

The rain becomes horizontal again.

It's her eyes that hurt the most.

A little after three, she wakes. She turns her wireless on for company.

She boils a kettle and begins unloading the dust from a dried-soup packet. She drops it into a filthy, cracked cup. She fills the cup to the brim. She waits for the magic mixture to froth into soup.

She picks up the steaming cup, takes it to the window, and perches herself on the ledge. She glimpses into the street. The rain is misty and blows sideways. She draws her first tentative sip of the gloppy concoction while the radio plays a hit-song.

She observes a family car pull up outside the elderly man's house. It's one of those cars that has bars fitted to the back. She recognises it straight away. The car belongs to the dog-man. The dog-man visits the old gent during the week. He arrives mid-afternoon to leave his boxer dog.

She sees the middle-aged, grey-haired, fawn-jumpered, dog-man hop from his car and go to the rear of his vehicle. She guesses the dog-man is about forty, maybe forty-five. He pulls his adorable puppy from the back. The dog-man strikes the dog with the back of his hand. The pet has a collar. He attaches a leash to the collar. He drags the dog down the red-tile path to the old man's front door. He rings the door-bell and he waits. There's no answer from within the house. The dog-man tries again. Still no answer.

So the dog-man leads his puppy to the front bay window and gazes through the nets. He bangs on the glass. Clearly, there is nobody at home. She guesses the old man must still be at the County hospital. Doubtless he's lingering in grubby corridors, along with other emergency patients, *yet to be seen.*

The dog-man returns to his car. He disconnects the leash from the collar. He urges his pet to jump in the back. She watches him make a call from his mobile phone.

The dog-man seems thrown by the absence of the old man.

She watches the car roar away.

2

Mrs Roylance is taken sick in the night — things look bad.

Mrs Soomro — the night manager at Clongowes House — calls Mrs Roylance's folks and tells them to *get to the home in a hurry*; though she already knows, even before she makes the call, they *won't* journey till morning. By then, it will be *too late*.

Mrs Soomro does the call to *next-of-kin* while Eimear sits and rubs her knees. Mrs. Soomro views her supervisor's calendar and asks Eimear if she'd *like to perform extra-duty*. Overtime at the care-home means getting the residents to the hospital in a Big Red Taxi. It also means sitting around and making small-talk so the oldie feels reasonably entertained while they wait several hours before they are seen. The care home prefers to pay extra money for night workers to stay on rather than use precious day-staff. Eimear agrees to help. The extra money will be useful.

Mrs Roylance's daughter reaches the county hospital just after eleven in the morning. By that time, Eimear has already been there half a day. She sits clear of the ward and reads a grotty paperback.

Her hair shines like egg-oil, her skin flakes like bad paint on a rusted radiator, and her pits feel vile and yeasty. She knows she looks a *right mess.*

Rising from a plastic chair, to greet the older woman, Eimear holds out her hand to deliver a face of sympathy. She explains everything that has taken place. Then she collects another plastic chair and places it alongside hers.

~

'My mother speaks highly of you,' says Mrs. Roylance's daughter. 'She tells me you are considerate...'

'That's good, thank you.'

'I guess you're tired?' Mrs. Roylance's daughter scans her unkempt hair.

'I'm a night worker at Clongowes. Last night, I didn't sleep.' Eimear rubs her eyes and finds an unexpected knot. She unravels it with grubby fingers. 'So, yes, I am dog-tired.'

'You must find this work challenging. You are required to be calm and pleasant 24/7. I don't think I could manage it.'

'What do you do?'

'I'm a manager in a big retail company.'

'That must be challenging *too*...'

'It's not like your job, though. You are required to be friendly at all times. Warm, caring, and approachable...'

'Actually, our job is mostly about being sincere.'

'I don't think I possess such qualities. I could never be sympathetic 24/7. I could never be considerate. '

'I'm sure that you *could*...' Eimear smiles. Then she adds, 'Our job requires stamina too. I'm the clean-up girl on nights, so I do all the sponging, swabbing, and wiping...'

'You've been so sweet to my mum ...'

'We have to be assertive. Often that's what's necessary.'

The women sit in silence. Mrs. Roylance's daughter glances at Eimear. 'What hobbies and pastimes do you have? I wish I had taken up needlework. My mother urged me to take it up. But I didn't have time. She was a wonderful crafter. Used her hands all the time.'

'I do online shopping,' Eimear says.

The woman laughs and she declares: 'You know what? You have a lot of common sense for a younger woman...' The doors swing open, and they watch two staff members walk towards their plastic chairs.

The doctor has a torn expression. The nurse stares at the floor.

Mrs. Roylance's daughter sobs before they arrive.

Eimear reaches home in Spring Lane. It's just after midday.

Outside, it remains blustery. She trudges along her side of the road, and she gets within a few yards of her front door, when she recognizes a familiar shape shambling along the opposite side. It's the mechanical tin-plate toy-soldier. He's marching along in his customary clockwork manner. And the old guy is carrying something.

Eimear decides she ought to go over just to say *hello*. She can use the excuse that she needs to tell him about the dog-man. She can say that the dog-man came visiting last afternoon, but he got no reply. Also, she's eager to know what transpired when the paper-boy went into hospital.

She checks for traffic, sees it is clear, so she stumbles and half-trips across the road in her bleary-eyed state. When she reaches the old man, she realizes he carries one of those deep-fried-chicken family-size buckets. *That's odd,* she reflects. The mechanical tin-plate toy-soldier doesn't strike her as a fried chicken *kind of guy*. And why does he require an entire bucketful? He lives on his own. Maybe he's having folks around for a party?

'Good morning,' she shouts as she closes the gap. 'I hoped to catch you before you reached home.'

The old man regards her with an air of uncertainty. As if she is about to do him harm. 'It's me,' she says with a smile. 'Don't you recall? I came to help you at the accident the other morning.

Eimear is my name. I live across the way.' She points to her window.

The old man arches his brow. He looks across the road and checks her building. 'I have to get inside,' he says. His eyes return to the chicken bucket. 'I cannot stand here...'

'Sorry...' she adds. 'I didn't mean to intrude.'

'Fine.'

'I just wanted to tell you that the dog-man came yesterday. While you were out.'

The old man clings to his bucket. He resumes a brisk pace. He is troubled by her interruption. She walks alongside for a few steps. He pauses anew, to squint her way: 'My son Nigel? He came to leave the dog?'

'I didn't know he was your son. The *dog-man* is what I call him when I see him from my window. I know he has a boxer pup, though.'

'Nice little friend he is — not the man, the puppy.'

'Yes. Well, anyway, your son knocked on your window — but he didn't get an answer. Because you were still at the hospital, I guess. With the paper-boy...'

The old man nods. He starts walking again. They reach his red-tiled path at the same time. She's at the point of saying, 'Well, I suppose you'd like to get indoors before the chicken gets cold...' but she hears him garble something in that bizarre, jumbled brogue that he uses.

'What?' she hears herself asking. 'What is it? What's the matter?'

'I need help,' the old man blurts. His eyes are watery. She wants to tell him she *needs her bed*. She wants to tell him she *hasn't slept a wink in 24 hours*. But because she's nosy, and she wants to know what's going on, so she says, 'What can I do to help?'

'Would you take the keys out of my jacket pocket?' the mechanical tin-plate toy-soldier nods to his left side.

She puts a warm hand into his tweed, and she rummages around a bit. She detects a cool metallic form and she pulls it from the lint. 'Are you going to do the honours?' he says. He nods at the key she found. 'I cannot put this down...' He shakes the chicken bucket.

She goes along the footpath first. He clunks behind. She unlocks the door and pushes it wide so they both might enter. 'Come in,' he says, 'Close tight behind. Might I ask you to help me?'

She wonders if he needs help with his overcoat or to take off his shoes. She's accustomed to facilitating old folks and she knows, for example, they have difficulty bending. That's what she does at the care-home where she works. She helps with their trivial things. She knows about their struggles. She knows it can frequently be too painful to budge open a door. Or pull off a sock. So she pushes the door shut for him and faces the old-man in the hallway.

'Can I trust you, miss?' he asks. 'I'd welcome guidance.'

'Of course,' she says. 'I'm happy to help.' She knows she must show strength of character *too*, so she adds, 'But only if I can. I'm awfully busy, do you see? So long as it doesn't take up too much time. I haven't slept all day. Do you see? I need to get to bed.' That's how she parleys with the residents at Clongowes House and that's how she talks to the mechanical tin-plate toy-soldier *too*. Because straight-talk is best when you're conversing with old people.

'What did you say your name was, miss? I y'ave forgot.'

'I'm Eimear from across the road,' she tells the dippy old man. He seems *extra* scatter-brained today. But she offers him a genial, but patient, smile.

'I'm George,' he pronounces, 'George Florn. I live alone. My wife died years ago...'

'Oh?' Is George looking for home help? Help with housework and what-not? Is that why the old man invited her in? He might offer a part-time job. Is that what all this is about? The extra cash would come-in useful.

'This is it,' he says. He hands her the chicken bucket. She takes it from him and gives a curious grin. 'What do you think?' he enquires. She hears a sound that comes from the inner recesses of the bucket, as if something moves *within* it. For a moment she thinks she might have imagined the crackle-sound, on account of her tiredness. 'I found it on the beach,' the old man continues to explain. 'I do not know what to do next.'

She gazes inside the bucket. It's *not* filled with food. There's no smell of fried chicken. In fact, it's not filled with anything much at all. Nevertheless the bucket has a definite *heaviness*. She inspects the top layer, and she sees a deposit of rubbish. Crap from the beach. She knows it's from the beach, because it has sand all over it. There's tinfoil and plastic bits. Some ugly things too. And they're all covered with damp sand and bits of grit. The top layer smells of seaweed. It's a stack of insignificant jumble that the old man probably collected on his walk along the coastline. Undoubtedly, the old guy is soft in the head!

Then it moves. The thing *moves*. Eimear reckons it's a *thing* that lays at the lowest stratum of the rubbish, beneath all the worthless crap that sits on top. She feels uncomfortable. Because she senses that something *breathing* down there. So whatever it is, it's not a crab! It's not a fish! Whatever the *thing* is, it wriggles, and it breathes! The *thing* inside the bucket is alive.

She doesn't have the courage to look deeper, so she returns the bucket to George.

'What is it?' she asks.

'It's a tiny, *tiny* baby,' he tells her.

'Sweet Jesus, Mary, and Joseph... we need to get this babby to hospital. For medical attention. Has the child been in the water? Did you say you found this scrap on the beach?'

Eimear grabs the bucket and holds it steady. She hurries to the sitting room. The mechanical tin-plate toy-soldier scuttles after her. She gets to her knees, as if she's doing her *examen* before Sunday mass. She places the sandy bucket on the magnificent, embroidered, cushion. She scoops the delicate bundle from the bottom of the wretched container. The baby's body under a layer of crud. 'For the love of God, George. What did you think you were doing? Fancy putting a babby in this filth? Are you out of your mind?'

The old man looks shamefaced.

She holds the infant to the light. The babe has a buttery-cream stain across its eyelids and dark-brown, wispy-black eyebrows. Sea salt crystals stuff the babies' ears. She wipes the grains of salt away with her finger. 'Quick, George. Get a blanket. And cotton wool. And warm water. Do you have a baby feeding bottle? Also a teat—'

George founders by her side. Then he dawdles off, to find what she demands.

'Don't dilly dally George,' Eimear shouts.

Eimear talks to the baby, 'Let's look at you...' She holds the baby to her cheek and feels the skin. The lips are split and there is gunk around the ears, but the baby breathes, and Eimear feels a bantam heartbeat. *Good God!* She holds the infant to her bosom and is comforted to find it makes minuscule, yet reciprocal, movements. Recalling she was once told that babies are inclined to female voices, she sings the '*Connemara Cradle Song.*' She gets to the line about '*calm be the foam*' when George returns with a blanket. 'Do you have cotton wool? Do you have the bottle I ordered?' she snaps.

'I do *not*,' he tells her. 'All I have is this clean flannel, here...'

'Give me that,' she instructs. 'Then make yourself useful. Call for a Big Red Taxi.'

'Big Red Taxi?'

'Yes. A Big Red Taxi. Good Grief, George, don't you know what a flippin' taxi is?' She shakes her head in disbelief and lifts a single eyebrow. 'Their number is on the business card in my bag. I left my bag by the door. Look for the card with the Big Red Taxi logo. Tell them to come right away. No delay.'

'Where are we going?'

'To *hospital* George, where d'ya think we're bloody going? You need to *get real,* for Christ's sake!'

They capably wrap the infant in George's best blanket. They take the Big Red Taxi to the County Hospital. They sit together in the back of the cab while Eimear cuddles the baby and George sulks.

'So you found her on the beach, did you, George, huh?'

'Her?'

'She's a little girl. Didn't you check? Jesus, Mary, and Joseph, are you away with the fairies today? Didn't you at least see the rosy bracelet on her little arm? It's one of those wristband bangles from the hospital. The nurses will know which hospital she's from when they see it. That will help us find her parents. They see lots of wristlets like hers —they'll be able to recognise it *immediately*. Maybe she got dumped by her parents? What do you think?'

The old-man darts a gaze, 'She was not abandoned — the tides dragged her in-shore.'

'Sounds unrealistic to me,' Eimear says. She sucks her top lip.

'However doubtful, it did happen that way, young miss...'

'Yeah?'

'I found her on the foreshore in drift and plastics...'

'Out sand-combing was you, George?'

'Yes, it seems very much improbable — but there it is...'

The old man fixes Eimear a solemn stare with steely eyes. She recognizes how wily he can be. He speaks again: 'She was floating in a structure made of bags and string.' Eimear pulls the baby close. The old man adds: 'Like a home-made life jacket for a babe...'

'Are you a beach baby?' she asks. She tenderly rocks the child. The baby doesn't open her eyes.

'I have the life-jacket at home if you need it...'

'I didn't see you carrying a life-jacket when I observed you in the street with the bucket...' suggests Eimear. She avoids his eye-contact and shakes her head. She knows he detects doubt in her voice. 'Neither was the babby in a jacket when I pulled her from that nonsense at the bottom of your container...'

'I put it inside my coat and the —'

Eimear cut him short: 'So you think she comes from a ship-wreck, do you George? You think the sea swept this babe overboard? You think she got tugged by waves and pulled by tide until she rocked-up in your chicken bucket, do you? Do you take me for a fool, George? Do you take the authorities to be fools? Don't you think you ought to offer a more acceptable explanation? My advice is to think up a plausible story, George, before we arrive at the hospital. Else the powers that be will throw the book at you. They'll want to know the whole truth, George. They'll want to know why an old man picked up a child. They'll want to know why a stupid old man picked up a child that doesn't belong to him. And frankly I'd like to know too! You had no right to do such a thing, did you? Am I getting through to you, George? Am I getting through to your thick old skull?'

'I know why you're saying those things, miss. But it happened like I said —'

'Oh? Where's the ship, George? Where's the report of a wreck? Why has it not been on the news? Why aren't cops and coast guards searching the beach? Why aren't there lines of good-folk, volunteers from town, combing the strand-line this very minute, with sticks and beaters?' She dipped her head toward the empty coastline as they passed. 'There's no one there, is there, George? It's as empty as your noddle.'

'So what do you think occurred, young miss? May I ask?'

'I think it's more likely the baby ended-up on the beach because a confused young mother left her there. Perhaps the young mother had been ill or medicated. Or drunk. Perhaps she was muddled-in-the-head and didn't know what she was doing. Or the young mother left the babby for a variety of other reasons. But, for sure, I think there's a young mum out there, right now, who will be sick with worry about her little girl. I think you ought to tell them a story like that when they ask. Or they'll think you're covering up all kinds of dodgy shit... don't you see that, George?'

'Would an anguished mother put a baby in a home-made life-jacket though?'

'As I say, George. Your account sounds crap. Think about it. Use common sense, for Lord's sake.'

At the County Hospital — Eimear's second visit in a day — they hurry to the reception where she orders George to 'take hold of the baby' while she checks-in.

Eimear removes her outer coat so staff will see her work uniform. She figures it will get them through the process faster. The neat blue uniform suggests she's a nurse. George takes the bundle from Eimear — but he seems flustered. 'Don't bumble George,' she nags, 'Take yourself and the babby. Go to that chair *there* — by the wall. I'll be back as swift as I can.'

He looks to where Eimear points and sees a large black woman seated on a screw-down plastic chair. The woman has a pile of shopping by her feet. 'What? But somebody is presently sitting there,' he explains. He shakes his silvery head.

'Yes, that's right,' Eimear replies with firmness. 'She is sitting there *now*. But you will get her to move. Because we need to be as close to those giant-flappy bronze curtains as we can, do you see?' George views a set of rubberised curtains at the far end of the room, near the screw-down chair. These are the drapes that separate the *seen from unseen*. The cloth that separates unsalvageable from salvageable.

George demonstrates his resistance to her request by arching his thick eyebrows. But he slopes off *anyhow*, tick-tocking in his robotic style to the occupied seat. Eimear delays going to the reception desk until she's sure the old guy is settled. She lingers to see how he handles the conversation with the large black woman who's already there.

When George arrives at the special seat, the one nearest the bronze curtains, he coughs. The black woman sees he holds a baby. 'You want for me to move?' she asks.

'Yes, in fact I do, Madam. I must sit there.'

'Thaws not a problem,' she grins. She gives his baby a quick glance and makes *coo-coo* noises. Then she hauls herself to tired legs and pushes her bags to another part of the zone. 'She's a perfect dabbling, is that one...' she comments.

Once Eimear sees the old man is settled by the curtain, she goes to the reception desk. The red-headed administrator checks a screen, writes a few notes, and soon enough, Eimear returns with a card. Eimear stands by George's chair. The old man tilts his head, like a gentleman, to offer her the seat. 'No thank you, George.'

'Don't you want to take the child?'

'Not now, George...' Eimear tilts her head. 'She's *your* responsibility, George. You need to get that into your soppy old head.'

Within minutes Nurse Rumjana pops a cheery face around the gap in the rubber curtain. She calls them forward. Eimear takes the child so George can get out of the chair unhindered. Once he stands, she takes care to hand the child right back to him. She decides George must be the one who has to explain what happened. They follow Nurse Rumjana into a treatment cubicle, behind the rubber curtain. The nurse takes the infant and places her on a trolley.

'She's a rare darling...' Nurse Rumjana says. She unfolds the wad. 'A little damp. Wet hair too, with reddened cheeks. No rashing, fortunately...' The nurse listens to the baby's breathing then checks her heart. She lays the babe onto her back to inspect the body. 'Not highly active, but regular and healthy.'

'In fact, we're worried she might be hypothermic. Also dehydrated,' says Eimear.

'She presents low energy levels, for sure, and she's unusually sleepy — you might be right. I'll take her temperature and see if I can find a rehydration kit. She has dry lips and dull eyes too. She's gone without liquids for a while, hasn't she? Can you tell me why? What are the circumstances? Why is she in this condition?'

'Go on George,' Eimear urges. She jabs her elbow into his ribs to get him talking.

'The tide deposited her on the strand-line...' George offers. He straightens to improve his poise. Eimear notices he places a balled fist into the small of his back to give himself strength. Eimear rolls her eyes and lets out a loud *tssk*.

'I'm not with you...' Nurse Rumjana declares.

'Washed ashore.'

What was the baby doing? Why was the baby on the shore?'

'We don't know...'

'Did she fall from a boat?'

'Probably,' George replies.

'But that's not conceivable, is it?'

'See, I told you it wasn't convincing, George...' Eimear says. 'I think it's more credible she got abandoned by her mum on the promenade. Isn't that more realistic?'

'Mmm,' Nurse Rumjana agrees.

'There's a wrist-band here. Some sort of hospital tag.' Eimear directs the nurse to the baby's bracelet.

'Oh yeah,' Nurse Rumjana examines the band. 'Not English. Written in Arabic. I don't recognize this. Not from an English hospital. I'll get it translated. I'll ask Nurse Barwaaqo to pop-in and see us. She reads Arabic and she might recognise where it's from...'

'I think fierce winds and unstable tides dragged ashore the baby...' George murmurs.

Both girls ignore him.

The nurse inspects the baby's bottom: 'Do you have an all-in-one? Plus a nappy?'

George and Eimear shake their heads.

'Bit odd, isn't it? To bring a baby into a hospital wrapped in a blanket, with nothing else. Not even a nappy?' The nurse frowns.

'Like I said, I found her on a beach...'

'Did you say she's *not* yours?'

'Nope,' Eimear replies. 'Lost and found...'

'Have you notified the parents?'

Eimear shakes her head, 'Not at this stage.'

'Oh, dear,' says Nurse Rumjana. 'I'll be back in a tick. I need to get a nappy and call a doctor. I need to take advice about this.'

Nurse Rumjana returns with Doctor Lourenço.

The doctor has brown eyes, and he smiles with bright teeth. The poor man looks dead on his feet. He notes the baby's heartbeat, then checks her breathing and body temperature. After, he turns to talk to them: 'I'm all out of rope today. Been hard at it, you see — a fifteen-hour shift.'

'Sorry,' George says, as if it's his fault. 'You must be exhausted.'

'Nurse Rumjana tells me you found the baby on the beach. Is that right?'

'Yes.'

'And you haven't informed the parents yet?'

'Nope.'

'They will need to be informed at once, of course.'

'Of course.'

The doctor checks the girl's limbs and feels her bones. Then he places her onto bent limbs and makes clucking noises. He pinches her toes and pulls a pen from a pocket to hold it by her nose. He moves the pen from side-to-side. Afterwards, the doctor wipes the tip of the pen gently against the baby's palm and he waits for her to grab it.

'Well, she seems fine, if under-nourished. We'll get her weighed and measured. How old she is?'

'We don't know...'

'Well, babies grow in unique ways, but some milestones are common. I noted she lifted her head and she turned it. So we can assume she's over six months. With her eyes open, she focuses on things like this pen. Also, see here—' The doctor pushes them closer so they might consider the baby's skull, 'The mastoid fontanelle is fused. We expect that to become fused around twelve months — though it can be earlier on some occasions. My guess is she's twelve months old. Although she looks far younger.'

'Gosh,' says Eimear. 'I thought she was a new-born...'

'No, she's absolutely *not* new-born,' Doctor Lourenço says. 'Though, because she's malnourished, and she's underweight. She has low energy levels too, and this has affected her bodyweight and condition. Underfeeding can lead to poor defence against infection, so we don't want her hanging around *this place* too long. It's not a healthy environment for a famished baby!'

The doctor examines the baby's eyes, then her ears.

'What's that yellow?' Eimear asks. 'I can see a yellow stripe that extends across her eyes and around her head. What is it?'

'I think it's caused by dryness. It doesn't look like a problem. I think it'll clear up in a few days. Malnutrition is caused by many disorders and even infection. But we are assuming this is caused by conditions outside your control? Am I right?'

'She was found on a beach...'

'I've been told that... I can't see signs of neglect — other than the *obvious one...*'

'Obvious one?' Eimear whispers. She flinches.

'Yes, slower-than-normal development. Over an extended period — outside your control, yes? How long has she been with you?

'Just a few hours...'

'Perhaps her rate of development is typical in her country of origin...'

'What country might that be?'

'It's hard to say. I guess from the physical characteristics she presents that this baby is of Middle Eastern origin. Or North African. I see they wrote the band on her wrist in *Arabic...*'

The cubicle curtain crumples-back to reveal an elegant nurse who looks like she might be Somali. She wears a groovy veil decorated with winged-horses. 'Halloo!' she says. She gives everyone an endearing smile.

'The baby must return for developmental tests, of course...' the doctor continues. 'But to be honest, the emergency room is *not* the best environment for her. I'd like to get her out of the hospital soon as I can. Once she's given rehydration. And once she's measured and weighed. We'll grab samples and release her today if that is okay with you both?'

They nod as they watch the Somalian nurse check the baby's wristband and attempt to interpret the Arabic writing. 'It doesn't look like any hospital band to me,' says the nurse. 'Just a name tag.'

'What's the name?' the doctor asks. 'Can we translate it?'

'It says *Amira*. There is no family name.'

'Amira?'

'Sweet, isn't it?' says the nurse. 'The name means princess...'

'Holy goodness,' says Eimear. 'Did you hear that, George? You found a princess! You found a princess on the beach.'

'The nurse will make notes and I will file a report,' Doctor Lourenço tells them. He prepares to go to his next patient.

'Yes.'

'The police have already been notified?'

'Er, *no...*'

'Well, they *must* be. We'll let them know. I will get reception to call them. The police will tell you what to do next. I will let you spend time in our cubicle until they arrive. Questions before I go? Any other advice you need from me right now?'

'No.'

3

An hour passes. They linger in the hospital cubicle.

Nurse Barwaaqo sees them. She says, 'Sorry guys, I have to turf you out. We need this space. Nurse Rumjana went to get a crib. We're going to place you by the wall, outside. Near the yellow chairs.'

A transparent cot is trundled into position beside Amira. The baby is treated to a side-brooched shirt with a clean nappy —both provided by the hospital. She gets placed into the crib by Nurse Barwaaqo. The nurse manoeuvres the crib to near the yellow chairs. She's trailed by George and Eimear. They sit on either side of the baby. They wait.

Eimear wishes she'd brought her music. Meanwhile, George cogitates about the cubicles. He notes eight separate units, each equipped with a gurney and other essential equipment. They utilize only six compartments, while two stay in a state of readiness. Patients spend 90 to 100 minutes in each cubicle. George calculates such things in his head. He pulls a notebook from his dusty tweed pocket, and he makes estimates and prepares drawings. Eimear doesn't understand what the old-man is doing. So she shrugs, then she pulls the anorak over her shoulders to keep away the chill. She feels sleepy, so closes her eyes.

An hour passes. Nurse Barwaaqo arrives. She shakes Eimear. Eimear stretches her elbows and rubs dirty fingers through strands of lank hair. 'What is it?' she asks. Her mouth feels dry. Her eyes are drained of vitality.

'The police are here,' the nurse explains.

'Oh God.' Eimear swivels her head to view the baby's crib. She tries to get her eyes to react. She's surprised to discover that George is awake. Though the baby sleeps.

'I didn't mean to drift off...' Eimear declares.

'No problem, honey,' says the nurse.

Near the rubber curtain stands a pencil-thin peeler. He has golden-coloured hair and wishy-washy blue eyes. He doesn't wear a uniform cap. They would be in proper regalia *back home*, she thinks. Not the English though. The English police are never properly dressed. The officer's hands are shoved deep into his pockets. He jokes with a nurse who struts past and gives him a coquettish wink.

'George...' Eimear yelps. 'The peeler has arrived. A young copper to see you.'

The old man stops drawing into his moleskin book. She sees charcoal stains on his fingers and makes out the sketch he did on his page. 'Save your book for now, George. Put your things away and pay attention...'

The old man does as he's told.

The sandy-haired peeler comes to Eimear, and he frowns: 'Are you reporting a misper?'

'Huh?'

The officer tries again, 'I said are reporting a misper? As in miss-sing per-son?'

'No,' Eimear shakes her head.

'Sorry, the nurse said you were. Do you know who is? I'm looking for some guys who are reporting a missing person? I am here to report a misper. The nurse told me it was *you*. Maybe I went to the wrong person.

'I am reporting a *found* person...'

'Found?'

'Uh-huh.'

'Oh? — it's actually the *same thing*.'

'It is?'

'Yes, both go on the same report, do you see? Both go on the exact-same database. They're treated the *same*. They match them up at the office. One person missing. One person found. Neat, isn't it? One and one makes two. Do you get me?'

'Good,' Eimear says, though she employs an uncertain tone. She opens her mouth to say something more, but nothing comes out.

The officer gazes at her blue uniform, then he smiles at her tousled hair. 'You a nurse?' His eyes gleam. 'Do you work nights? You seem exhausted, love.'

'No, I work at Clongowes House. It's an elderly care home on the edge of town. I take care of residents...'

'Oh, sorry...' the officer says. He carries an air of disappointment in his watery eyes. The officer sits on the final yellow chair, and he stretches his long neck, to gaze at the old man. 'This is *the one*, is it, love?'

George fixes his stubborn eyes on a remote object and refuses to return a glimpse at the peeler.

'Is this the one you found?' presses the officer. 'We get a lot of them wandering. Did he escape from Clongowes? This the one you're banging-on about?'

'Escape? Er, *no*.'

'Yes, we see this a lot. We get a lot of escapees. He seems weak in the mind, if you ask me. The old git is suffering Alzheimer's. Poor old sod. Same thing happened to my uncle... just the same way as this. The senile old bugger couldn't even remember his own name. Mind you, my uncle was thick as a brick *before* he got that way. But age got him in the end. He finally went *radio rental*. Like this one...' The officer rotated his index finger near his skull, demonstrating his uncle's *radio rental* state-of-mind.

'You've got the wrong end of the stick...' says Eimear.

'What do you mean?'

'It's the baby'

'What baby?'

'It's the baby in the crib. She's the one that's been found.'

At this stage, the officer notices the wheeled bassinet parked between them. 'So the old man has nothing to do with it?' he asks.

'He has *everything* to do with it...' Eimear says. She yawns.

'What do you mean, love? You'd better give me the complete story.'

The officer pulls a notebook from a black pouch while Eimear stares at his name-badge. She tries to make sense of the words on it. He wears his name-plate upside down and even if it were the right way up, it would be tricky to read because the letters had been rubbed away.

The peeler gazes to where she studies, and says: 'Constable Brewhouse. That's what the badge says: Brewhouse.'

'Cool. Did you know it's on upside down?'

'Looks fine to me.' he says. 'Right, where do we start?'

'Er?'

'First things first,' says the peeler, 'What is the missing person's full name? '

'Huh?'

'Sorry, *sorry*. This is a found report, isn't it? These are tricky things. Because they're the same thing, love, do you see?'

'So you said.'

'What is the full name of the person found?'

'I don't know.'

'You don't know?'

'Incidentally, it wasn't *me* who found the baby. It was the old man...' Eimear tilts her head. 'The old gentleman's name is George. In case you require it for the report. He says he found the baby on the beach. You need to record that information. You ought to be talking to *him*.'

Constable Brewhouse glances at George and he shakes his head. 'Not now...' he says, 'Leave the old gent out of things. I'd rather talk to you. He doesn't look *compost mentis*, if you know what I mean. Plus, we don't want to over-tax his delicate mind, plus *plus* it's a long way past his nap-time...' The young peeler laughs at the joke then stares at his pocketbook. It remains empty. 'Right. Where were we? What is the full name of the missing person?' You tell me all the facts, please, because you more are *compost mentis* than the old-timer, yeah?'

'I don't know.'

'That's unusual. In my experience, people usually know the name of the person they're reporting missing.'

'But this is a *found* person...' she says. 'Do I need to remind you? I doubt people, by-and-large, know the name of the person they've *found*. Surely a found person is someone who is unfamiliar to them. That's just an assumption, officer, but all the same, I think I'm right.'

'Maybe I can leave a blank space for now. Hopefully, the computer will allow a blank space instead of a name... So what do you know about the person who's found?'

'Her first name is Amira. She is about twelve months old.'

The officer scribbles something into his book.

'Anything else? Like: do you know her date of birth and full home address?'

'Not really...'

'Family name? Next of kin? Place of birth? Anything like that? All those facts are required. We need to match this kid with other missing nippers in the area. Do you understand?'

'Nope.' Eimear rubs the back of her neck.

'Oh well, what's the description?'

'Baby-shaped. With brown hair and dark eyes.'

'Height?'

'Hold on — the doctor gave me a form with data on it.'

The peeler seems pleased with this news. At last he'll have something concrete he can write into the empty spaces of his report. He grabs the doctor's form enthusiastically and he copies down the facts. Once completed, he returns the form.

'Right. That's about it. Just your details now. Name and address?'

Eimear provides her name and address, but there is a note of restraint in her voice.

'Anything the matter?' the officer asks.

'I think you should take George's details, not mine. He's the more important witness here. Not me. He's the one what found her. He has the *vital* information. I'm just here to help.'

'Like I said, let's leave the old-boy out of things, yeah?'

'OK, so.'

'That's all then?' The officer puts his notebook away. 'Are you Irish, by chance?'

'I am. Did you tell from my accent?'

'I've an aunt over in the bogs. I've been out to her cottage. Scatty as hell. Aren't they all, though? The Irish I mean. Doolally, to a man. She lives in a lovely place, mind. It's very rural. And, yes, they're all scatty. Though they're not as bad as people think.'

'There's not much work on the Isle,' Eimear suggests.

'Still.'

'Don't you want to know where the baby was found? Time and place? All that?' she asks.

'I thought you said they found her on a beach?'

'That's right.'

'This morning?'

'Yep.'

'I have all the information, then. It's in the book.' The peeler taps his pocket and moves to stand.

'Is that it?' she asks.

'Yep. That's all there is from me.'

'Do I need a reference number or something?'

'I will not get a reference number until I put this onto the system. You could try calling the station later if you need a number.'

'No, that's fine.'

'You know my name, anyways. If there's anything else, just call...'

'Yes. And will the social services be informed?'

'Once I get back to base, I will put the report on the system. I'll check the box for social services. Or is it uncheck the box? Anyway, whatever it is, check or uncheck, I will do it... I will make sure they are informed... They generally get informed, *anyway*. I think they get informed automatic. Yes, that's it. They get informed automatic whether I check the box or I don't. Or is it the other way around? I think they get systematically informed, anyway. So don't worry.'

'Will the social services come and take the baby?'

'What?'

'Will they take the baby?'

'Why would they take the baby?' The officer becomes serious. His silly smile leaves his face.

'I don't know. I just thought they might come and get the baby from us.'

'Why would they do that?' The officer gives her a double-take. 'They'll be informed *automatically*, like I said. I suppose they'll decide later.'

'Oh, right so.'

'It's the mother you see....'

'What is?'

'She's the one who will be in trouble, if that's why you're concerned about. It's not *you*, is it? You've done nothing wrong have you? If anything, you rescued the child. Didn't you?'

'Yes. Well. Not me, but...' Eimear points to the old man. 'He did, anyway.'

'Like I said, when I get back to base, I will file a report. It will be cross-referenced to the missing person. We'll put two-and-two together and *hey presto*, we'll have a match. You won't have to wait long for the result.'

'How long do you think it will take? To get a result, I mean?'

'When it's on the system?'

'Yes. How long will it take to get the baby collected once it's on the system?'

'No more than a few hours.'

'So what do we do now?'

'Go home. Get sleep. You look shagged... sorry love, bad choice of word, but you know what I mean...you look absolutely *fu*—'

Eimear cuts in: 'Should we take the baby with us?'

'Of course you must... that's a strange question...'

'I thought we'd be passing it onto someone, that's all...'

'Like whom?'

'I don't know. Like social services, I suppose.'

'Didn't I already explain that? I thought I just went through the procedure...'

'Yes, you did.'

'You take the baby home. Get rest. We've got all the details.' The officer taps his pocket-book again. 'In a few hours, you'll get a call to say the mother is on her way. She'll collect the baby. They'll be reunited, mother and daughter. Big successful conclusion. Lots of tears. Lots of kisses. Another song and dance with a happy ending.'

'Great.'

'Like I say, the social services might want to look at her at some stage. Ask how a child of her age got herself abandoned on a beach, that sort of thing... but it's not really something *you* need to worry your head about, is it?'

'I suppose not. Thanks.'

Constable Brewhouse has all the material he requires for a report. The peeler brushes his uniform with his hand then routinely tugs a smartphone from his back pocket. Eimear is positive there's more to say, but the constable looks at his mobile-phone screen and grunts, 'I have to make a call...' He steps aside.

She imagines he's about to update his control room, presumably to keep them informed of events and to circulate details of the foundling baby. But, *no*, he's not. 'Hello love, you, okay?' The police officer makes a playful grin towards Eimear. Then he realizes she's listening to his private call, so he turns his back to continue with his chatter, 'I can't talk right now...' he mumbles. 'I'm at the hospital dealing with a missing person. I'm over-heard by a scatty Irish nurse. What? Yeah? Huh? Oh, yeah.' The constable moves a few steps, and he rocks on his feet while he natters. Eimear listens to his side of the conversation: 'Yeah, it's been quicker than expected. I'm calling to say we can get to your cousin's after-all, yeah? The sergeant has allowed me two hours' time off. You'd better get ready, yeah? I'll be home soon. We'll get going right away. It's about an hour's drive, I think. The forecast is heavy showers. No, I can't see anything from this dump. There are no windows in a hospital, are there? They don't want the old 'uns gasping in bed to see what they'll be missing when they croak, do they? It looked overcast when I came in, yeah. So bring an umbrella. Yes, I love you too. Right, cuddle-buggy, got to go...'

The officer slopes away.

Eimear checks the baby. The baby is asleep. She examines the old man. The old man sits motionless. He wriggles the end of his nose like he's dealing with a pong. She wonders why the elderly fool did not fall asleep like she did. She notices his eyes are sharp and they are unusually bright. Eimear says, 'You did not help much, did you?'

George turns his head, and he scans her face, 'I think you handled it well without me, young miss.'

'Well, to be fair, George, I hoped you might chip in. I hoped you'd pipe up when it came to your turn. But you sulked, didn't you? Not a single grunt from you all the while the young peeler was here. What got into you? Why didn't you back me up, George?'

'The lad was going through the motions. It's all he did.'

'Still, my dear, you might have supported me, don't you think?'

'The officer didn't give a sheep about our child...'

'She's *not* our child, George. I don't need to remind you of that. Also, don't forget I only came here to help. This mess is something you got yourself into. It has *nothing* to do with me.'

'I apologize. Sorrrrray. You did all right...'

'So you think the peeler did a perfunctory job?'

'Needless to say, he wanted to rush things. Get away.'

'So he could get to the party?'

George nods.

'Well, don't just sit there, dear. You'd better call for the Big Red Taxi. We need to get home.' George gives one of his inscrutable expressions. Eimear clarifies: 'You'll need to take my phone outside to make the call. You know how to use a mobile phone, don't you?'

George provides a thumbs up sign, and he gets to his feet. His shins look slim. His knees are shaking. His left leg reels a bit. He places a rigid arm behind his back, and he stands tall, like a stubby, mechanical robot. It's the way he holds himself.

Eimear digs out her phone and she switches it on. 'You'll have to leave the building to get a good signal,' she explains. 'I stored the number under Big Red Taxi. Get them to come *right away*. I don't want to stay any longer than we must.' Eimear opens the screen and passes him the handset. 'Get on with it, George. Don't dilly dally...'

She watches the old man scuttle through the electric doors. Then she turns her attention to the baby.

On the return trip Spring Lane, Eimear cradles the baby and whispers to George: 'We need formula, nappies, wipes, bibs, separates, a sippy cup, sterilizer, and a bottle.'

George considers this statement. His bushy eyebrows twitch when she says the word, *we*. The temples on the sides of his head move. One after the other, they move up and down. They bounce like a pair of swing-levers. He moves his buttocks to the same rhythm and produces a soft brown leather wallet. 'Do you think this will cover the items you yen?' he asks. He pulls a crispy fifty from within the folds.

Eimear ogles the banknote as if it were a sacramental offering, then she snatches it from his bony fingers before he can put it back. 'It will suffice, George. Do you have any more of those in your purse?'

The old man opens his wallet to expose half a dozen fifty-pound bills.

'Good,' she says, 'Because we'll need to pay the driver when we get back home. Plus, I'll need additional money, for sundries.' She looks sharply into the old man's geriatric eyes.

The Big Red Taxi approaches the down-town Metro shop.

'Stop outside the grocery...' Eimear yells. The driver nods and he pulls the cab inwards, onto zig-zag lines.

'Now wait here,' she instructs. 'George, take care of the baby, while I go look for essentials.'

'How long do you think it will take to get all the odds?' the old man asks.

'These things take time, George,' she says. 'Don't fuss. It will take as long as necessary.'

Eimear steps into the fuzzy rain. She thinks it will *piss* soon. 'Stay here, driver,' she shouts. She zips into the store.

∾

Back at George's place, they pay the taxi driver and they take the baby in.

Eimear arranges foods for the baby and she places her on a towel, on the bathroom floor, to change the hospital nappy. She tells George to study because he'll *have to do this task himself.* George remains in a reluctant slouch, by the door. The old man revolves his shoulders while he watches.

Eimear hands George a baby feeding bottle and says he ought to take the child to the big chair, to let her drink. She notices he handles the baby properly, although he takes the bottle, to splash liquid on his arm.

'What are you doing? *Don't* do that...' she scolds. 'It's unsanitary. Sometimes I don't understand you one bit, George. One moment you are sensible, the next minute you are an *absolute* spanner. Wise up and sort yourself out before it's too late.'

George takes the child to the main room. Eimear puts away the items she bought. She places the bits into neat cupboards. Then she goes to find the old man. To judge how he is doing.

George is doing well. The baby gurgles, satisfied.

There are small-scale models around the room. Each model sits inside an individual glass home. She wants to know what those miniatures are.

'They are the chief patterns I made folk over the yonks...' George tells her.

'Patterns?'

'Yup.'

'But patterns are decorations, aren't they? Like swirls on the wallpaper?'

'Patterns are designs. Pattern are replicas of larger objects.'

'So you made these models did yourself, did you George? You must be good with your hands. You must be a real craftworker...'

'Tharr not models, they're patterns... As I told you.' His shaggy brows upswing with displeasure.

'What's the difference between models and patterns?' Eimear asks. She stifles a yawn. She knows she's becoming wilfully quarrelsome, but, frankly, she's doing it simply to stay awake.

'Models are replicas of things that yarr completed beforehand,' the old man says. 'Patterns are replicas of things yet to be built.'

'I see. So, all these little things have grown-up equivalents in the real world?'

'No.' The old man presents her with a grimace. He clacks his teeth. She supposes the noise implies he's *more* nettled than he was before.

'No?'

'Only *some* are made into the full-size thing they represent. And, like I told you— they yarr *not* models. They yarr patterns...'

'Why only some?'

'Some projects never make it. Don't get accomplished. Get killed off. Some projects do not grow into big things.'

'Why are you so grumpy, George? You need to lighten up.'

'I yam not grumpy. I like to be precise, is all.'

'Sometimes I find you're a relatively wise old man... then, at other times, I find you're a total *plank*. Admit it, George, you are a confused old plank, aren't you?' She says this as a compliment. But the old man doesn't reply. Eimear guesses she's been too tough on him.

George checks the baby, and he pulls away the bottle.

'You never told me what happened to the newspaper boy...' she announces.

'He brook a choker bobe,' says George.

Eimear shakes her head because she's puzzled. She knows the old man speaks English, but it's not the kind of English she is used to. It's no type of English she's ever heard before. George points to his neckline. He tries to explain: 'Nasty shock. Broke 'is clavicle. Took to hospital... that you know.'

'What happened after?'

'His parents arrive late, waited until they sawed him...'

'You performed first aid...' she declares. 'That impressed me. Where did you learn first aid?'

'In yarmy. In Royal Engineers. Way back.'

'Of course,' she grins. 'I thought so. I knew you were an army soldier. I worked it out from my window. You enjoyed being a squaddie, did you?'

'Not much. Just yan engineer doing National Service.'

'How long?'

'Two years...'

'Is that right?' Eimear nods her head. 'Is the Army where you learned to take care of yourself? Is the army where you learned routines? Is the army where you learned to keep fit? Is the army where you learned to sketch hospital booths? '

'I suppose *not*. It was when I became a patternmaker that I learned most things.'

'I see.'

4

Eimear returns to her bedroom at the normal hour. She is drained of energy. She sits sideways, as always. On the ledge, where she rests her weary back-bone *every* morning. She waits for the old man to emerge and begin his daily exercise. Regular as a cuckoo-clock, she *knows* she can depend on him.

He'll stand on the porch, and go through his routine. It's an everyday habit he *never* misses. Neither does she! Eimear scans the street for any runaway paperboys. There are none today, the street is deserted — though the thoroughfare will soon be full of movement. The wind reduces in strength. Eimear watches the sky. She decides it will be silvery-dull day.

She checks the watch on her uniform and thinks about the previous 24 hours. She didn't discuss her day's escapade with anyone at Clongowes. She didn't tell them about the old man named George. How he'd found a babby — found a tiny baby on the beach. She didn't explain how she went to hospital. Again! How she fetched a constable. She didn't discuss taking the infant back to the old man's home. Why would she?

Where is he?

She knows the old man is a slave to schedule. He's a creature of routine. Typically, he's at his door-step *by now*.

A bubble of acid rises in her stomach. She promises herself a mug of lukewarm soup *later*. Her eyes sting like crazy. Her tongue feels dry. Her toes are concrete, 'Oh God, Jesus, Mary, and Joseph...' she says out loud. 'He does not come... it's the babby. Something is wrong with the child. I must go see.'

She throws her thin anorak around bony shoulders and collects the phone from where she tossed it — on the candlewick bedspread. She squeezes her toes into clammy pumps and exits her bedsit. Eimear creeps the staircase and makes it to the hallway. But before she reaches the front door, she hears a faint click. It's Mrs. Slaviaro — the proprietor of the house. Mrs. Slaviaro comes from her chambers to learn where her house-guest is going.

Eimear offers Mrs. Slaviaro a generous smile. Mrs. Slaviaro stands in a nylon robe, wrapped around bent shoulders. Her yellow flip-flops are decorated with plastic marigolds. But Eimear can only concentrate on the ugly corned-beef feet that jut from those marigolds, and the woman's cracked heels that look like enormous white cliffs of cheese.

'Where you off to, young lady?' asks her landlady.

'Huh?' Eimear dips a chin to avert the woman's gaze.

'I thought you told me you worked nights? I thought you told me you slept all day? You been coming and going all hours, these last days... haven't you? What have you to say for yourself, young lady?'

Eimear wants to tell Mrs Slaviaro to *shove off*. She wants to say: 'What does it matter to you? It's none of your business. What do you care? I'm not your daughter. I'm a paying tenant. I'm an adult. I can do *whatever I want*...' But Eimear does *not* say any of these things. She bites her tongue. Because it's difficult to find inexpensive accommodation in a coastal town, especially on the south coast. And particularly if you are a single young woman and equipped with an Irish accent.

Eimear chooses to humour her landlady. She says, 'Sorry missus

— I'm doing a swift errand. It won't take a tick. I'll be back in a wink. Then to bed. I promise.'

'Well...' says the older woman because she hasn't finished her admonition. 'I need to give you a *piece of my mind*...'

Eimear cuts in quick, to avoid unpleasantness. 'And how are you, missus? You're looking fine and healthy this morning, so you are.'

The woman crumples her nose at these words. It's as if she's dealing with a dreadful aroma: 'They told me I shouldn't trust an Irish...' she prattles. 'They were right.'

'What do you mean?' asks Eimear. 'Why can't you trust me? I don't think I missed payments, did I?'

"No, you didn't. You'd better not neither, or I'll have the law onto you.' Mrs. Slaviaro sniffs. 'I'm talking about your Fenian ways. You say you're running errands — but I know where you're going.'

Eimear shrugs.

'You're going to visit the tin-plate soldier, aren't you? Like you done these last mornings. Don't deny such a thing...'

Eimear is tempted to say, *what if I am?* But chooses to ignore the comment. She stifles a yawn.

'Of course, it's none of my business...' continues the meddlesome ratbag. 'But it seems foul to me. *Foul*...'

'Okay, so —'

'Dirty language, evil practices, wicked habits — that's the Irish. *They* told me that. I should have listened. I ought to have taken *their* advice. I didn't. Unwise of me, wasn't it? Still, I know better *now*. Never trust an Irish.'

'If you say so, ma'am...'

'Well, hurry along then,' Mrs. Slaviaro says. 'Do your foul deeds. Off to grab the codger's life savings, I suppose.'

'Hmm?'

'Also, just so you are aware...' continues her landlady. 'My accountant advised me to carry out a rent review. I'm sending letters to all my tenants. You'll receive your notification shortly. It will advise you of a rent *rise*. A rent-rise you won't be able to afford.' The old woman *harrumphs* at this. She turns to retreat into her rooms, to feed her green parakeet.

'Silly cow,' says Eimear, under her breath. She releases the latch to step into fresh morning air.

Eimear hurries across the way — to visit the old man's house. She frisks along his crumbled red path and rings his door-bell. No answer. Should she go to the front bay window and bang? Knock loudly, like the dog man did the other afternoon? She doesn't need to do more, though, because she hears a raking sound. Then a long squeak from the hinges. The front door is loosened, then it is thrown wide.

'You're late...' she says. She squeezes past the old man to get into the house... she needs to hasten because she knows her landlady will be watching through the front nets. Eimear tugs the door closed.

'Nothing's amiss young lady,' says the mechanical tin-plate soldier. 'I just put the baby down...'

She glowers at the old man. She furnishes him with a most unkind glare.

'To answer the door' he explains.

'Is she well enough, though? Is she? I had a terrible fear she was not well. Tell me she's fine, I beg you...'

'She's fine and dandy. A little zappier today.'

'Where is the babby? You should not have left her on her tot.'

'I yam sorry.'

The old man takes Eimear to the main room where he has placed the baby in a cradle. The makeshift cot is basically a drawer that he's taken from an old piece of furniture. Eimear *tuts* when she sees the state of things. 'This will not do, George. I don't know how long we must keep her — but we can't have Amira sleeping in a box, can we?'

Eimear takes the baby from the improvised cradle and gives the child a hug. Seeing the babe's sweet coppery cheeks and sensing the warmth in her scrawny body, Eimear feels overcome by relief and utters an involuntary whimper. She pulls herself together quickly: because that will not do — *not do at all!* One must be strong. One must be strong in the eyes of the elderly and infirm. One must *never* present emotion to a senior resident.

'Well...' Eimear says, after a sniffle, 'You've done well.' She wipes her eyes. 'I shouldn't have snapped. For that, I apologise.'

The old man places a comforting hand on her shoulder. 'Want a coffee?' he suggests. 'Can I get you something?'

'I'm fine, George. I have not slept for days. Too long. I need bed. That's all. I think I'm burned out.'

'Yes, of course. I can deal with things here. May I see you later?'

'Yes, of course. I will be over once I've bedded myself for a few more hours. You take care of this little one *until...*' Eimear passes Amira to the old man. They saunter to the front door. 'Did you change her?'

'Yes, I changed her *twice*. Once in the night and once now...'

'That's fantastic George.'

He nods.

'And, George, we need to buy more stuff —'

'Do we?'

'First, we need to buy a baby carrier. Something like a papoose. Once we have an item like that, we can go for a walk. I mean, all of us. All three. Along the beach, *together*. Like a family.' The old man's eyes glisten like sequins on a ball-gown. 'I want you to show me *exactly* where you found her.'

Eimear wakes after three, later than she would like. She boils the kettle but feels excited. She doesn't need soup. The old man's house is uppermost in her mind. She needs to get over there right away. The baby needs to be checked.

Because she's running late, she's worried that the dog man might already be at the old man's address. She remembers the dog-man's name. It's Nigel. He comes most weekdays. It's approaching the time he usually arrives. Eimear pulls her work clothes on. She checks her phone is fully charged. She picks up her keys and slips out of her room.

She slinks out of the house. She dashes across the road to ring the old man's door-bell. This time she's patient. George arrives soon enough. He's holding the baby. Eimear goes in.

'I wanted to get over to your house before the boxer-dog man arrives. I'm sorry I overslept...'

'I rang and told my son *not* to come. This mite comes first.'

'Why did you do that, George?'

'I need not explain. He's my son and I will do what I need...'

'Okay,' she says. She rubs her chin and gives him a sideways glance.

'I'll explain things later when I judge how best how to say what needs to be said...' he clarifies.

'Fair enough, George. Another question: Why does your son leave his dog with you?'

'He goes to the gymnasium to do haerobics...'

'Aerobics?'

'He pulls weights and so forth.'

'OK, so.'

George puts a bent fifty-pound note into her hand while Eimear sweet-talks to the baby. 'For thee to buy the girl a pouch,' George explains. 'Like you say what we need...'

'Of course. My mind went blank for a second. May I use your loo?'

George shows her the way to the downstairs toilet. At the door he lingers. He says, 'Do you hanker for a yopen sandwich? I have one about now, each day...'

'I don't know what an open sandwich is. What are you talking about George?' Eimear is about to go through the toilet door, but the old man delays her progress. She narrows her eyes into slits. Then she takes *a tone* with him: 'Do whatever you like, George. But move *aside.* Let me get into the loo. You're getting in my way... don't get in my way. *Ever.*'

'Sorry. A yopen sandwich is a slice of butter-bread with sprat and tomato, you see.'

'Yes, I would like an open sandwich. But stop hindering me. Stop being so flipping disorganized. Stop being so bizarre, frankly. Really! It's distressing to find you so muzzy-headed! I thought you'd be a well-organised gentleman. But you're quite the opposite, aren't you, George? You are utterly chaotic. It's maddening. Quite maddening! Get out of my way. I will meet you later when I've done my business, *heavens...*'

George gazes at the baby but continues to prevent Eimear from entering the bathroom. The old man provides a pensive stare. The silly old-fool is conflicted. 'You can leave the tot on her own while you're making a sandwich...' she explains. 'It's fine to leave her for a *moment.* Just don't leave her too long, that's all...' George gives her a meagre smile and removes his foot. He takes Amira, to put her in the makeshift-cradle. Then shuffles to the kitchen. To fix their sarnies.

George arrives in the main room. Eimear curls on the couch. She seems content. The baby bubbles and rollicks in the pull-draw crib. Eimear takes a willow plate from George and munches her snack *immediately.* It's gone in two gulps. She's famished. When she stops eating, she stands to brush the crumbs away, 'I must get going...' she suggests 'You want me to buy the baby-carrier?' She produces the fifty-pound note from her blouse. 'It's a fair way to the shops, George. We might not have time for our walk. Not today. Sorry to disappoint you. I don't think we'll have time for a walk...don't forget I work nights.'

'Take the bike...' says George.

'Which bike?'

'The paper-boy's two-wheel cycle. I got it in the back.'

'You still have it? The bike he crashed? Yes, I suppose you must. I thought it was all smashed up, George? It is, isn't it? It got mangled in the crash...'

'But I fixed her up. She's good as new, isn't she?'

'Did you? You fixed his bike? When do you have time to fix a bicycle when you're caring for a babby 24/7?'

'During the night. I worked on her then... before you camed back...'

'Didn't you sleep?'

'The tiny one. I had to check her every half hour... so I didn't sleep yet did I?'

'Oh, George...'

George leads Eimear to his workshop. It is a lean-to, fixed to the back of the old house. It is accessed by a rear door. It smells of oil and glue. In the centre of his studio, resting on a special rack, sits a shiny bicycle. 'But George this can't be the same bike! No, surely it cannot be the same one? This bike is brilliant, George. This bike is *gleaming*...'

'I painted her up didn't I? And straightened her forks,' George provides a proud grin.

'This is incredible.'

'Will you take her to the shops? Much faster on this...'

'What about the paper-boy? Will he mind if we ride it?'

'He'll not use the bike till they fix his bones, will he?'

'I suppose that's true, he won't. That's a good point, George. He'll be happy to see his bike in this condition when he's fit and ready to collect it. Me-oh-my, wow, you did an amazing job on this.'

Eimear wheels the paper-boy's bicycle to the front of the house, and she sticks the fifty-pound note into the cup of her bra. She starts for the shops. But before she goes, George comes to the front-door with a big chain, and a giant padlock attached to one end.

'For wellbeing for when you leave it at the roadside...' he tells her.

'Of course.' He passes her a little key. She sticks the padlock key into her left ballet shoe.

~

The toilet water stench of the sea strikes her nostrils as they approach the coastline. It is late afternoon, and they must hurry. Eimear only has an hour to spare before she begins night work. She finished the shopping in a trice, to cycle back on the paper-boy's mended bike. She purchased a wrap-style carrier for the baby. Now they walk at the beach with Amira in the wrap. The clouds that once moved lazily across the sky now congregate in a mean muster. Like the yobs in the town-centre, they grow rowdier by the minute. The bleak sea is green, and boisterous too — the result of a ripening tide.

Eimear views the rubbish and assorted debris scattered all over the strand-line. It's a twinkling mixture of crud. Bits of useless plastic, no longer desirable. Washed-up and clogged-up *chaffy*. The plastics are bundled with filaments of seaweed. The bits of crap look like parcels left by a demented mermaid.

The old man walks nippy on a twisted path. He leads the way to the foreshore. He takes this walk every day. 'When you stray from the path, try to dodge oil and mulch,' he suggests.

Eimear puts her hands under the new baby-sling, to offer further strength for the infant's weight, especially now they pass from smooth surface to crinkled jumble, underfoot.

Eimear studies the strewn litter.

George tells her there is *nothing to find most days*: 'But sometimes I hook a nautical treasure,' he suggests.

The baby struggles to focus her eyes on a seabird that passes overhead. But gives up and squeezes her mind shut. Eimear wipes salt from Amira's eyes.

'When I pace, I keep my heart-wide open,' the old man continues. 'To see things for what they are... I find the beach is the best place to think.'

'What do you think about?' she asks.

'Life, relationships, patterns.'

'How stupid to abandon a valuable thing to the sea,' Eimear says. She stoops to view an expensive footstool that's overlaid in salt-stain and now sticky with gastropods.

'Sometimes surrendering is not a choice,' the old man continues. 'yielding is the best chance of escape...'

Eimear doesn't know if George is speaking about the footstool; or about himself. So she sniffs and shakes her head. She thinks the sea looks like a gigantic, muscular creature with innumerable cobblestone eyes and hefty haunches. 'I like the brine...' she says, as if she's reciting some kind of prayer to baby Amira.

'One day the joy you deserve will foam into life,' the old man adds. He points to a spot where Eimear already identifies a bigger than average mound of gunk. 'That's where I found the mite...'

'What brought you to this spot?' she asks.

'Glass shards. They glinted near...'

'God.'

'I picked 'er up and saw 'er gasp...'

'How do you know this is *specifically* the spot you found her?' Eimear looks about. The beach looks the same everywhere. 'It could be *anywhere*... I don't understand how you could know you found her here exactly.'

'I found a point of reference. That lighting rod *there*...' The old man points to a dishevelled building. Eimear glimpses it in middle-distance. A dilapidated amusement arcade. On the apex of the roof, she sees a narrow spear. 'I got orientations from that yonder thing. I recorded my steps back to the esplanade. An average step is thirty inches. I know this is the exact spot where I found 'er.'

'How do you know such things?'

'Doesn't everyone know?'

'Er, *no* they don't George.'

On their return trip home, George points to Eimear's lightweight slippers. She wears them on damp feet, without socks. She examines her toes and sees they are soaked and filthy.

'Do you need new shoes? Can I get you fresh Mary Janes?'

Eimear considers the crackled, tattered, flats: 'They're manky I know,' she says. 'But I'll manage. Thank you, all the same. You do *not* need to buy me gifts, George. I'm not the one who requires charity.'

The old man dips his head to demonstrate he understands.

'Should we call for anything for the tiddler, though — I'll let you know right off... is that fair?'

'Right-ho...' George says. He presents a tolerant smile.

'Actually, I'll call social services when we get back...' Eimear adds. ' We need to get ourselves an update.'

'Very well."

Indoors, George carries the baby to the bathroom to change her nappy. Eimear uses the landline in the hallway. She doesn't know the number for social services but finds a number listed under social care in an enormous book the old man keeps under the hall table. Eimear calls this number and is put through to an automated switchboard. She chooses from a list of overwhelming alternatives and picks one that purports to be the *office for child protection and safeguarding*. They transfer her to another number that goes straight to another patch-board. Eimear remains on the line to talk to someone because that's what the automated-voice promises. The robot says she'll be put through to a 'single point of contact.' After a dubious click, she hears a woman giving a long and weary sigh before uttering something incomprehensible. Then Eimear hears, 'How can I help you?' though she notices the woman's words are given a testy tone.

'Yes, I will tell you,' Eimear says. 'I'm trying to see if you have an update on our found child.'

'Found?'

'Yes, she's been reported *found*. I'm looking for an update...'

'What's the reference number?'

'I don't have a reference number...'

'What's the name of the case worker?'

'I don't know. That's why I'm calling you. I'm trying to get information...'

'How can I help if you haven't got a case number? Call back when you have all the facts to hand. If you call back with all the details, plus the name of your case worker, maybe I can help.'

Sensing the woman is about to ring off, Eimear shrieks: 'It's an emergency. It's a police matter. Can you look it up for me?'

'Well, just a moment.' The council-worker sounds fractious.

Eimear wraps the phone cord around her hand and smiles at George while he brings forward the baby.

'Hello?'

'Yes, I'm still here...'

'Do you have the full name of the found person? We can check our records if you have a full name and date of birth...'

'I don't have a full name...'

'Look, I'm sorry, miss. How can I help you? You need to call back with the *correct* information. Call another time. A better time It's not convenient to chat with you *now*, because this office is about to close. But when you call back, I advise you to provide the case reference number and also the full details of the found person. Agreed?'

'But I ...'

'Good day.'

5

'Miss Yemarr,' George says.

Eimear smiles because it's the first time the old man has ventured to use her name. 'I wonder if I may prevail upon you?' The baby paws her arm. The infant spent the morning with the mechanical tin-plate toy-soldier before Eimear arrived. Eimear turned up at the old man's house just after two. 'I have to go to the grocery stores. For provisions.'

'Of course,' Eimear says. 'Do you want me to stay and watch the innocent?'

'I commonly shop each day. I lack bare essentials...'

'Where are you going?' she asks. She believes the old man will say *the superstore*. But he says, 'The fish market, the fruiterer, also the baker...'

'And the butcher too?'

'I do not eat meat ...'

The disclosure surprises her. Aren't old folks renowned for their love of bully beef, ham-bones, and gravy? She didn't figure George as a veggie. 'Are you vegan?'

'I abstain from meat but eat eggs, fish, and dairy products,' he clarifies.

'Cool.' Eimear doesn't know what else to say.

'We can go jointly. Just the market and the shops...' the old man suggests.

'I don't know, George. It looks damp outside. We don't have a waterproof jacket for the babby. Not *yet*, anyway...'

'I'm suggesting it might be workable. That's all.'

'We could wrap her up warm, I suppose.'

'They cast her in the sea. And she survived, didn't she?' he comments.

'How long do you think we'll have to wait?'

'Care after the little one, you mean?' he asks. He squeezes his sliver-bark eyebrows together.

'She's no trouble...' adds Eimear. 'I'm not suggesting she is any trouble. I enjoy caring for her — really! Don't you? But I get anxious about her mother. I'm worried the baby's already been with us *too long*. And why haven't the authorities sent someone? Why haven't they been in touch?'

'I don't know. She's no trouble, is she?'

'No trouble at all...' Eimear smiles at the baby as if she might understand. 'But I've been thinking — it's not likely, is it? All that *lost at sea* tripe. It's far more probable her mum abandoned her on the beach, isn't it?'

'I showed you the exact place yesterday, didn't I?'

'Yes, you did, George. You showed me *a place*. A place of grit and pebbles. I thanked you. It's all very well, George, but it doesn't prove she went overboard, does it? It got me thinking: what became of the mother? For example, how come the authorities haven't found an adult washed onto the beach? Would a mother allow her baby to go in the seawater and not follow after? I'm fearful, George. I'm fearful about the fate of the mother. What happened to the woman? Maybe she had a carry-on with a man she didn't know. Or got assaulted. Or maybe her man was unhappy, or she got plugged by another. Or it could be a hundred different other things... all hideous. Do you see? If it's true the baby went over the side, it brings more questions, doesn't it? But if, as I suspect, the mother just abandoned the girl on the beach, then the mother must be *somewhere*... and by that, I mean somewhere *nearby*. Somebody *should* know something... shouldn't they?'

'I see.'

'It is all extremely complicated, isn't it, George? It's terribly complicated, and it's making me feel frantic with worry. This situation could even involve *murder*. Jesus, I hope it doesn't, but it *might*. Don't you see, George? That's why you need to be clear about your story. I want you to get your head right about it. I'm worried about Amira. I'm more worried about her mum. I'm worried about you, *too*, George. How the authorities will deal with you over this. Mostly, though, I'm worried about what became of the babby's Mum? It's a mystery, isn't it?'

'The best way to allay your fears is to call police...' the old man suggests. 'See what they done and what they're doing.'

'I'll ring them when you're out shopping. If we find the baby has to stay with us a few days more, it won't be a problem, will it George? But we'll need to more equipment for her, yes?'

'I almost forgot...' George says. 'The little miss. She started to crawl today. She has her strength back...'

Eimear gives the infant a little squeeze and says, 'Who's a clever girl, then?'

The baby mumbles an answer.

Eimear places two large bath-sheets on the hall floor to shield the carpet. Then places baby Amira onto the towels so the little-one can crawl around to her heart's ambition. Meanwhile, George prepares for his shopping expedition.

'Do you want to take the bike?' she asks. 'It will be much faster...'

'I'm no good at cycling...' the old man says. 'I tend to fall off.'

She laughs as the old-soldier plods the garden path, scarf wound tight around scraggy neck, cocoa-coloured brogues meticulously laced onto comically small feet, and a hilarious lounge-hat settled on his fluffy soft hair. Once George is out of the door, Eimear collects the phone book and finds a number for the local constabulary. She calls the number she finds and starts a lengthy process. She aims to hunt down Constable Brewhouse.

After several minutes of transfers, shifting responsibilities and infuriating dead-ends, she gets through to someone who sounds like they *might* be able to help. It's a young-sounding female in the police control room.

'I'm trying to contact Constable Brewhouse. He's an officer with —'

'And you are?'

'My name is Lambe. Miss Eimear Lambe.'

'And what's this in connection with?'

'A found child.'

'Wait. I'll see if the officer is on our system...'

The line goes dead.

'Oh no, not again,' says Eimear. The baby crawls to the front-door then stops. The baby gazes at the door as if she's contemplating a reverse journey.

The phone-line fizzes back to life, 'PC Brewhouse you say?'

'Yes, I —'

'Wait.'

Two minutes later, the female voice returns. 'We cannot raise him on the radio. I'm just looking to see if he's on duty. *Wait.* Checking the roster for you now.'

'Thank you,' says Eimear, to a silent line.

The line sparkles back to life: 'The officer is not answering his airwave. We think he's on duty. But later. We might recommend you try calling back...'

'Do you think I could leave a message?' Eimear asks. 'Only, I'm experiencing trouble getting hold of this policeman. I keep getting caught in dead-ends.'

'Didn't Constable Brewhouse leave a direct number for you to call him on?'

'No, he never.'

'Let's see if we can email him... what do you want to tell him?'

'Please tell him to contact Miss Lambe, *urgent*. Tell him this is about the child that has been found. He can contact me on this number. Or perhaps at this address. I'll be here all afternoon. I leave for work at five.' Eimear provides George's land-line details and the old man's address.

'Okay,' says the female voice at the control room. 'Everything is sent. By email. Is there anything else I can help you with today?'

'No. Thank you, you've been most helpful.'

Eimear returns the handset to its Bakelite cradle then crouches to confront the baby on the floor: 'Things are advancing...' she tells the little one. 'Would you like to see your mummy?'

The baby gazes back and dribbles.

At around half-three Eimear hears a car pull-up outside George's house. 'Goodie — the police are here...' she says to Amira. She lifts the baby from the impromptu play-mat and brings her into the back room where the makeshift cot is ready. She puts the child down for a nap. Then there's a steady knocking at the front door.

'We have a bell, you know...' she says. Eimear shouts, 'Coming...' then she hurries to the hall to open-up. As she prepares to turn the handle, she brushes herself down and picks imaginary cotton-tufts from her unwashed hair. She gets ready to give the police constable a trusting smile.

She opens the door to greet her visitor — but, *no*, it's not the person she expects. It's *not* the policeman. It's Nigel, the forty-ish year-old dog man. The guy she *now* knows is George's son.

'Hello,' Eimear says, a-dither.

Nigel seems equally confused. 'Hey, er — is my father at home?'

'No. He went to the shops...'

'Really?'

'Uh-huh.'

'Might I come in and check?'

'What do you mean *check*? Don't you believe me?' She opens the door wide so Nigel might enter. But she offers an irritated scowl.

'It's not that I don't believe you, love —' returns Nigel, the boxer-dog man. 'It's just that I don't know *who you are*. It's odd that my father should be out. He has a fixed routine. Do you see? He *always* follows a fixed routine.'

'I'm Eimear...' she explains. 'I'm from across the road.'

Nigel, the boxer-dog man, closes the door. He ignores what she says. He examines the hallway, and he asks: 'Is he in the workshop?'

'Nope! Like I said, he went to the shops...'

'Anyway, I had better check.'

'Suit yourself.'

Nigel makes long steps towards the back of the house. The girl follows. He unlatches the workshop door, and strolls in.

'Hmm. He's not here...'

'Like I said.'

'This is odd.'

'Is it?'

Nigel pooters back to the front door again. He has an aimless way about him that, for some reason, she interprets as mean-spirited. His attitude unnerves her. Now she sees him close-up she reckons he's forty-five, with squidgy hair, waxy skin, frosty eyes, and he's about six feet tall... she decides he *must* take after *the mother*. Because he'd tower over the poor little *papa*.

'Do you mind if I ask who you might be?' he says.

'Me? I already told you. I'm the girl across the street.'

'What are you doing here?'

'Minding the place while your father is out...'

'Do you know who I am?'

'Yes, your dad spoke about you...'

'Hmmm.'

'Where is your dog today?' Eimear seeks. 'Your Dad told me you leave a boxer while you go training...'

'In the car... I wonder why my dad hired a cleaner? He never told me anything about hiring a cleaner.'

'A cleaner? I'm *not* a cleaner. As far as I know your father *hasn't* hired a cleaner.'

'What are you if not a cleaner? I detect an Irish accent. What are you? A home help? Why are you in our house?'

'A neighbour. I thought I already explained.'

'Oh yeah, from across the street...' Nigel, the boxer-dog man, shakes his head as if he doesn't believe a thing she says. He presses his lips together.

'Yup.'

'Well, anyway, my dad goes shopping on weekday mornings. He lives life as regular as clockwork. He uses a chart. Did he show you his chart? His chart will say morning shopping. In fact, his chart will tell you he makes tea around *now*. His tea is *always* an open sandwich. My father adheres to a strict timetable. I doubt he has changed his schedule in years...so why has he changed it today, I wonder?'

She shrugs: 'Right so...'

'I wonder why he is suddenly changing his habits? I wonder why he needs someone to look after our house? I wonder why he needs home help? I wonder why he has gone out in the afternoon? I wonder why he has started to do things he has never done before?'

Eimear contemplates an answer but doesn't know whether she should tell Nigel about the foundling baby *yet*. She decides *not* to, at this stage, unless he asks. 'It's just *today*...' she offers. 'I know he'd typically shop in the morning. But your dad found himself short of provisions...just today.'

'Did he? That seems unlikely. He knows I come the same time every day. I come around *every* afternoon. Why would dad go out when he knows I'm coming? It makes little sense. And another thing... he's ignoring my phone calls... Strange things are happening.'

'Oh right.'

'I think you're to blame — *somehow*.'

'Me? Why? What did I do?'

'I don't know at this stage, but I mean to find out.' Nigel, the boxer-dog man opens the door and he readies to leave.

'Well, thanks for popping by then...' Eimear says. She provides a perfunctory smile.

'Look, love, cut the crap, yeah? Tell my dad when you next see him, that *I'm onto him.* Tell him I'll be back. Tell him I demand answers. Tell him I need to talk to him about the mess he's getting himself into.'

'I will.'

'Good day.'

When George comes back home, he has a clutch of shopping bags. Eimear informs him that his boy called.

'What did he say? Did he ask why I was not at home?'

'Why haven't you told him about the baby?' she says. She gives the old man a cross look.

'I didn't think he would understand. That's why...'

'But he's your family. Don't you think he deserves to know what's going on?'

'What was he like about you being here? Was he nice?'

She wants to declare *lukewarm.* But that would *not* be true. *Antagonistic* might be a better word to describe him. Instead, Eimear chooses another word altogether: 'Perplexed.'

'I see. I yope he wasn't impolite to you dear...'

Eimear shakes her head.

'I'm sorry if he was —'

'Oh no, of course he wasn't impolite,' she confirms, in a scolding tone. She crosses her arms and juts her chin: 'He was as polite as anyone might expect... he found a strange person in the family home and the presence of the stranger startled him. He didn't know what was going on. Doubtless, that's because *you* haven't explained things accurately yet, have you, George? So it's *your* fault, don't you see? I completely understand your son's confusion. I'd be just as puzzled as the same thing had happened to me. Anyhow, he said he'd call later, to discuss things with you.'

'Amen to that,' whispers George. 'I'll be glad to have a chin-wag.'
'For sure.'

The following afternoon, at three o'clock, Eimear darts across the road to ring at George's door. The old man opens after a while. His face is filled with vexation. His eyes seem *dampy*. She asks, 'Is anything the matter? Is the baby okay?'

'Nigel wants to come over to tidy affairs...'

'I wonder what that means?' she asks. She pushes, to get herself inside.

The old man delivers a dismissive shrug, once she's in the hall.

'Where is the babby?' she asks.

'In 'er cot, snoozing,' replies George.

'What time will your son come round?'

'Don't know. Soon, I think. His normal time.'

'Well, don't worry. I'm sure the whole thing will go fine.'

'Oh, by the way, Miss, do you want a key for yourself?'

'A key?'

'To enter solo. When I'm busy with the baby. Like now.'

'I see your point,' Eimear says, 'But I don't know. It wouldn't be right, would it? It wouldn't be the done thing. People might get the wrong idea. They might think it unseemly.' However, Eimear realizes the old man's idea has merit. It would mean, for example, she could slip in promptly without her nosy landlady spying from across the way. 'Yes, okay, but only temporary, George... until we resolve things with the babby.'

'Agreed.' George says. He hands her the front door key. He has tied a strand of green cord to one end.

'Thank you,' Eimear says. She puts the key under her bra-strap, green tuft exposed. 'I'll boil a kettle...' She steps towards the kitchen. 'To make a nice cup of tea... would that be a clever idea? I expect you'll need a cup...'

'Make a pot. It will be thirsty work. Me and my son...'

The doorbell rings. George goes to answer. Eimear hears hushed tones from the hallway while she prepares tea in the kitchen. She listens to heavy toes crunching on carpet. She supposes Nigel, the boxer-dog man, will head to the living room. She waits, to allow things to settle, before she takes in a pot.

Eimear pushes the door open and introduces her foot into the room, Nigel *immediately* expresses displeasure: 'What are *you* doing here?'

'I want to introduce you properly. This is *Yammarr...*' says George.

'We've already met...' mutters Nigel. He shuffles his feet grumpily. 'I thought we were going to conduct a *private* conversation. *Private!* Without strangers eavesdropping on every word...'

'Do you want me to leave?' Eimear asks.

'No,' says George.

Eimear regards both men. She chooses to remain. 'It's his home,' she declares. 'If George wants me to stay, I'll stay.'

'It's George now, is it? God, give me strength. You aren't even trying to hide your intentions anymore, are you? What a skank! It won't be his home for much longer, will it? Not now you have your scrawny bones in the door and your claws into his feeble mind.' Nigel gives a hateful stare.

'What is *that* supposed to mean?' Eimear says. She slams the tea-tray onto the side table with a thump. Then she crosses her arms and makes a face.

'You know very well what it means...'

'No, I don't... if I *did*, I wouldn't ask...'

'Now, Nigel...' says George. 'Surely we can get along together.'

'Really?'

'That's no way to talk to my friend. She came to help—' adds the old man.

'Help *herself*, more like,' says Nigel. 'I came to talk *about* her. Not *to* her. Are you going around the bend? Why did you invite this little vixen into our home? Have you gone weak in the mind?'

George does not respond. Eimear thinks the old man resembles a dead guppy, with a vacant mouth and melancholy eyes. 'Maybe I should go...' she offers.

'No, don't bother,' says Nigel. 'It's *me* that should go. Clearly, I'm not wanted around here. I thought I might be able to give valuable advice to my father. But I can't do it with *strangers* intruding.' Nigel stands to leave.

'Nigel, don't be like this...' expresses the old man. 'We're trying to tell you something *important*.'

'It can wait,' says the son. 'Whatever news you have, will keep.'

'But...'

Nigel stands to move to the hall. Eimear allows him to pass unhindered. That's when the dog-man glimpses the bit of green cord poking from her bra-strap. 'My God...' he barks. 'Have you *utterly* lost your mind?' He gapes at his father. 'Have you given her the spare keys to the house? Mum's old keys?'

'Convenience...' George replies.

'This is the giddy-limit! This little trollop comes over here and she sweet-talks herself into your life — and what do you do? You give her the bloody front-door key! You air-headed old fool... this is utter *bollocks*.'

Nigel marches to the hall. As he strides, he continues to holler: 'I'll be back when you're ready to talk... and I mean, talk *alone*. But now I need time to think.'

They see the walls shudder as he smashes the door shut. Thhey hear his car growl away.

'I'm sorry, Miss. I truly *yam*.' The old man looks at her with pity in his eyes. 'Since a lad, he's been angry. Do you have a brother, Miss?'

'Just a sister. Older than me.'

'And your daddy? What does he do?'

'He drinks.'

'No, I mean, what does he do all day?'

'Like I said, he drinks.'

'About my age, I suppose?'

Eimear throws her head back and she laughs: 'No — he's half your age.'

'And your mother? What does she do?'

'She's given herself over to the parish...'

'Very praiseworthy,' the old man remarks.

Eimear sees how the glossy surfaces of his eyes reflect the feeble light of the afternoon. 'Don't get mawky on me, George.'

'Mawky?'

'You know what I mean, George — you're becoming maudlin. Cut it out!'

'I miss my wife, you see,' he explains 'I wish she was here. She'd know what to do.'

Eimear decides it's *not* time to show any weakness. So she tidies things and takes the crockery to the kitchen. She leaves the old-timer to fork through his memories. Alone.

'Any news from the police or social services?' Eimear asks, when she returns from the kitchen. She anticipates the old guy has composed himself.

'No,' George the old man states. 'But I phoned the Maritime Gendarmerie.'

She glances at George, bewilderment in her eyes. 'I don't even know what that means...' she mumbles. 'Please explain yourself.'

'The French coast guard,' he tells her.

'Really? Why should you do such a thing?'

'They might help trace the boat that left their shores.'

'Oh George! Are you still on about that?'

'They suggested —'

'George,' Eimear says, cutting in. 'Answer me this and tell me *the truth*. Did you *actually* find the babby on the beach? '

'Yes, I did. You know I did.'

'Do you really think she was washed here? Do you really think she fell overboard? Do you really think that someone, conceivably her mother, didn't try to rescue her? Do you really think, against all odds, the babby survived hours in the ocean? So do you really think she drifted here? To be picked-up by you?'

'I do,' George says.

Eimear studies his eyes and sees he suffers the same illogical, but *deep*, conviction that her mum suffers when she's talking about *her friend* Jesus. 'In that case,' suggests Eimear, 'I will go along with your yarn. For your benefit. And I promise I will not question you any more about it.'

'Thanks,' George says. He achieves a fragile smile. 'The French coast guard will get back to me with data...'

'Right, so. In the meantime, the British authorities are not working as fast as their French counterparts. It looks like we're going to be with the tiny-one for a few days more. We need to get more stuff.'

The old man is pleased by this news and offers an elated smile.

Eimear continues, 'I will call for a Big Red Taxi and you need to go and find some of your larger banknotes. We need a proper cradle, a play-pen, more nappies, an outdoor coat, and...' So Eimear begins to make a list while George scuttles off, to accomplish his responsibilities.

George, Eimear, and baby Amira take a Big Red Taxi to the superstore. At the entrance, Eimear pays the driver and tells him to come back in an hour.

They mingle with other shoppers at the side entrance, trying to locate one of those carts that's likewise a baby organizer. George puts a pound coin in a slot to free their chosen cart from a chain. Eimear tips the orange paddle-seat flat so they can happily plonk the child on board. They make their way into the large, bright building.

Eimear suggests they go *immediately* to the top floor where the home, clothing, and household items are located — so she pushes their hand-cart onto an inclined walkway. George grips the rail as tight as he might. She glances back and thinks he looks like seasick teddy bear! Once they show up on the top level, Eimear leads them through shiny aisles to the baby goods section — past strollers, dressers, changing tables, car seats, and toys. She stops at the clothes section to look at a long rail of colourful anoraks.

'Also, we need shoes,' she says, flicking the rail.

After a brief interval, George goes off on his own to explore. Eimear tracks him from the clothing and watches the old man heading for a display of electronic goods. It seems he's looking for child monitors.

'George...' she calls, 'Don't stray! What colour coat do we need for the babby? This peppermint green looks nice...'

The old man scuttles back: 'Yes, very nice...' he declares.

'What were you doing over the other side, George? I need you by my side. Please don't wander off.'

'I was looking at baby yalarms...'

'We don't need one, do we? She's almost twelve months...'

'It would be extremely useful.'

'Come on, why?'

'I could work unbroken periods in my workshop... and listen out for her.'

'The machine monitors breathing...'

'But I will hear her if she cries. Or needs food or changing.'

'Well, it's your money, George. I can't stop you; I suppose. But I think it's a waste. Get one if you want, but I warn you, they're not cheap. Are you sure we need one?'

'It will be yelpful in the mornings while you're asleep...'

'In that case, choose one that uses a technology they call D.E.C.T. You do not have Wi-Fi, so that's what you'll need instead. Also, you don't need video, so find a box that tells you it monitors *audio only*.'

George wanders away to look at the boxes again and see if he can see the unfamiliar word that she pronounced as *decked*. Eimear smiles at the baby: 'You'll help me shopping, won't you?'

The baby bubbles.

George bends his ancient knees. Then he narrows his old eyes to scrutinize a box he's found. He decides it requires further checking. He struggles to slide the box from the others, then rises to tiny, unbalanced, feet. After the rise, he comes over all muzzy and Eimear sees him wobble back. He splutters, steps the wrong way, and then accidentally strikes a passing lady who's with her pushchair.

'Mind where you go...' the woman snaps.

'I yam sorry,' George says politely. The old man lifts his hat. He looks at the woman's infant, seated in the stroller. 'How old is your little one?'

'It's nothing to do with you...' the woman says. She pushes her kid away and gives him a definite snort. George seems nonplussed by the woman's manners. Then he grabs his chosen box and brings it closer to his nose to read the fine-print written, in yellow, on the side. The light is inadequate in his area, so George moves further from Eimear to a place where there's more light, thrown by high tubes.

By his feet shoots a small girl. She plays with a plastic dolphin. George smiles at the child and pushes her away from his legs. A fractious mother sees this act and pulls her girl away. The mother guides her child to another part of the store. George continues to read the box. Satisfied it's the right product, he returns to Eimear's side to place the box of micro-electronics in their trolley. He rubs a wrinkled hand across their baby's forehead. Amira looks up at and smiles. That's when a bloke in American-style security uniform comes over to clutch George by the elbow: 'I'm sorry sir, I must ask you to leave...' the security man is no older than twenty-five.

'But why?'

'I insist...'

'What have I done?' asks George.

'There have been complaints.'

Eimear shakes her head to express her disappointment in George. She says, 'Really, George. I can't take you anywhere. We'll catch up with you outside. Go with the security officer now and try to be commonsensible.' She continues to shake her head.

'What have I done?'

'No matter...' she says. 'Before you go, though, may I have money?'

George looks at the pile of baby products in the cart.

'How much is your gadget?' she asks.

'Thirty.'

'You'll need to give us two big notes then.'

'Sir,' insists the security man, even though George is passing his wallet to Eimear.

'I'm coming...' the old man says.

They escort George from the store. A group of young mothers watch the procedure. They smile a victory smile. They have triumph written generously across fat-creamy faces.

George and Eimear stop outside the superstore and wait for the Big Red Taxi to return. The old man cradles the baby in his arms while Eimear takes their special trolley back to its proper place. Afterwards, she returns to replace the baby into their carrier-sling.

'Delightful scene,' says a mature lady. She is wearing a brownish hat. She watches as they sits on an adjacent bench in the bus shelter. She has heaps of shopping around her feet. 'May I ask, are you the great-grandfather? I suppose you must be...'

George gives the woman a confused smile. He shakes his snowy-white hair. Eimear sits alongside, with baby Amira, so the lady in the brown hat continues, 'I was just saying to your great grandfather, my dear, you don't see many older men out shopping with their family. I was just remarking it's a lovely scene...'

'Right so,' says Eimear. She decides the relationship between her, George, and the babby is too convoluted to explain to all-and-sundry, especially in two minutes at a communal taxi-bus stop. So she looks away to wipe snot from the baby's nose.

But the woman in the hat persists: 'So is daddy at work? Does your baby take after the baby-father, or take after your father's father? Sometimes they jump a generation, don't they? It can be queer, can't it? Queer? I mean queer with regard to genes. ' Eimear nods. 'And what does he do?' asks the inquisitive woman.

'Who?'

'The baby-father? Well, he's not here with you, is he? So it's a fair question, isn't it? Where is he? He works, I expect. Yes, that's what it must be. What does he do for a living?'

'This and that...'

'And how old is your baby?'

'About twelve months.'

'About? Small though! Looks younger. A prem? My sister had a prem. They can be tricky little sods, those prems.' The woman's eyes follow the contours of their baby. She lifts from her seat to peek into Amira's face and give them the benefit of *yet another* of her opinions. Promptly, though, she responds to the baby's dark skin and brown eyes. The woman makes an odd throbbing noise in the base of her throat, then she slams her rump back down onto the plastic bench. Eimear sees the woman grown inwardly grouchy. The woman squints at them, her eyes resembling two creases in a crinkled pillow. The woman then provides her with an extremely disappointed look.

'Well, it's not mine...' says Eimear with a wave of hand.

'It's none of my business...' replies the lady with the hat. 'What young people do these days is none of my business. I feel sorry for the old man *though*...' The woman looks at George, then she shakes her head. 'What must he think? Fought for king and country. What for? For this? Like I say, none of my business, but he must be ripped up inside... the poor old bugger, he must be *ripped up.*'

'It's none of your bitchness —' Eimear mutters.

'Well, I never. Whatever next? What a rude little girl you are. No wonder you can't find yourself a white man.' The lady lifts her shopping bags to the far end of the taxi rank to distance herself from such disgraceful people. It doesn't matter, because their Big Red Taxi arrives.

'What's up with her?' George asks.

'Who knows? She's just an onion-skinned gas-bag."

When they get home, Eimear changes and feeds the baby while George hurries to his workshop to play with his new baby alarm gadget.

She's eager to know what he's doing stuck in his workshop for *ages*, so goes to find out. He has unpacked the baby monitor and now reads an instruction book. His nose is pressed to the pages, working under a heavy work light.

'Written in French, Deutsch, and English...' he tells her. 'I yam reading it in *French*...'

'Awesome,' Eimear says, although she offers an apathetic shrug. 'What's on the wall? A new plan? It looks like a coloured-in map, like the ones we had in geography classes, when I was twelve. I don't remember this map. Is it new? Something you're working on? A design for one of your models?'

'It's a plan of the Channel, from Cherbourg Peninsula...'

'A map of the sea?'

'I'm tracing the boat's course. To find Amira's parents... I have calculated tides and currents.'

'Gosh. What's the model you're working on?' She examines his workbench. She views a freshly built miniature that might one-day go into one those little presentation cabinets. This new model looks like a row of honeycombs.

'Polygonal tessellation. For the hospital...'

'Whatever is that? I don't do big words.'

'A design for a new emergency department.'

'Who told you that you could design a new emergency department?'

'Just a little fun.'

'Never mind all that, George — come and see the baby in her new cradle.'

Eimear urges the old-man out of his dusty workshop. He brings one part of the baby monitor with him. Once they get to baby Amira's room, the old man connects the transmitter into an available wall socket. The apparatus lights up right off and seems to work. He wants to give it a test. 'Say something...' George suggests, 'Once I yam out of the room, though.'

Eimear hushes her voice, and, when she reckons he's far enough away, she whispers: 'Funny how a baby can start things up. How a baby can give direction to a life that turned meaningless...'

George returns and gives her a thumbs up.

'Did you hear it?' she asks.

'Like crystal,' he says. He presents a hesitant grin.

They admire the baby's fresh new clothes. They watch how she snuggles into her soft modern cot. At that precise moment, Eimear has the overwhelming urge to clasp the old man's warm hand, or at least put her arm around his silly, scrawny shoulders. But, of course, *she doesn't*. Such a thing would *not do*. It's not sensible to get attached to senior residents. They're not around for long. It's best not to get too melancholy, either. So, instead, Eimear softly rubs George's left shoulder. She says: 'I'd better get away. I'll be late for work.'

6

'The hospital telephoned whilst you have been *ya-sleep...*' George relates this news as Eimear lets herself into his front door, the following afternoon. The old man had apparently been waiting in the hallway, with the baby, for that precise moment.

'Hospital?'

'About the development clinic we must take her to.'

'Have they given a date and time?'

'Monday at ten.'

'Holy Mother! Sure, she ought to be off our hands by then?'

'I don't know.'

'Any word from the police yet?'

'Nope.'

'I have to go back to them. I might attend the station to speak to them in person.'

'If you phone now, I'll make a sandwich for our tea.'

Before they begin, a car pulls up outside and they put all plans on hold. George walks into the front room, to see through the net curtains. Eimear follows.

'Is it the police?' she asks.

'It's my son Nigel,' George says with a frown.

'Oh hell,' Eimear says. 'If he finds me here, he's sure to go through the roof. He'll turf me out on my bun... that's for sure. He'll give you a roasting *too*...'

'Go to my workshop. Hide there. I'll show him the little one, and I'll explain everything.'

So Eimear skulks to the rear end of the large house. She opens the latch to the old man's lean-to studio, and she enters his private world. She looks at the coloured map pinned to the wall. Then checks the models on the desk before she finds herself a wonky stool. The front-door is unfastened, and she listens for male voices. She looks around for something to read. 'I hope this won't take long,' she says.

Eimear settles with her backside on the stool, then picks up a crackle that comes from somewhere under the work-bench. She hears disconnected voices, too. And these voices, though ghostly, sound close. It's only when she dips low, to peek under the bench-top, does she comprehend what's going on. The mysterious echoing noises are coming from one end of the old man's new baby monitor.

'I found a baby... I want to show you. To explain,' she overhears George telling his visitor.

'What?' says the other voice. She presumes the other voice comes from his son, Nigel, the dog man: 'What's a baby doing here?'

'I'm looking after it...'

'Well, it needs to go... Get rid of it.'

'I can't right now. Don't you want to see her face and her little hands?'

'No.'

'Why not?'

'Have you gone crazy?'

'I found her on the beach.'

'You did *no such thing*.'

'What do you mean?'

'It's hers, isn't it? This baby belongs to that girl. This baby belongs to the trollop you gave mum's spare keys to...'

'The girl?'

'The Irish.'

'No. It's the baby I found on the beach t'other day...'

'This is intolerable. You install a floozy into our home. A floozy with a kid. And now you expect me to go along with the lies? You allow a stranger, an Irish slattern, into our family home... and welcome her baby too? Are you utterly, utterly, mad? You are becoming an irresponsible old man and I think *this time* you've gone thoroughly potty...'

'It's not made up...'

'Did the girl bring the baby?'

'No — like I said, I found her on the beach. Washed up there.'

'I've had enough of this.'

'Can't you see I have a drama here? I need help...'

'You need help for sure — you've lost your marbles. You need to see a doctor. We need to get you looked at. You'll need a proper psychiatric assessment and probably they'll lock you away... in a secure unit... for your own good. I can't have you risking our inheritance, this property, all our heirlooms, and my birth right, all your savings, by your reckless stupidity and this feeble-minded indiscretion...'

'What do you think I should do? Give me your advice...'

'Kick *Miss Nibs* out of our family home, for starters. She should take her stinking bin-lid with her. Tell her to sink back to Cork or wherever else she climbed out from... Tell her to keep out of our life... Tell her to wind her neck in. Tell her to keep her nose and her thieving hands out of our investments and fortune.

'But —'

'This won't happen again if you get yourself to the quack for a mental health evaluation. Ask if your doctor can do anything about your dementia. The first step is to admit you have a problem, dad! You have to admit it: you are going senile.'

'If you cannot help, I'll ask your sister for advice.'

'You will leave her out of it... do you hear?'

'Why?'

'She's a long way off. Leave her out of things. She's made a stress-free and uninterrupted life for herself. Why would she want to endure this utter nonsense?'

'It's not nonsense...'

'This has come on truly fast, dad. I don't know what to think. You were right-as-rain just the other week. Yet *now* you've nose-dived into decline. They say senility advances slowly, or so I've read, but for you, the onset of dementia is happening extremely fast.'

'So you won't help?'

'My chief concern is the girl. The Irish hustler. She is bamboozling you. She inveigled her way into our home. And now she has eyes on our loot. Don't you see that?'

'She didn't inveigle. I asked her to come help me out.'

'You *think* you asked her because you've become deluded. Don't you get that? She is duping you. You are being *used*. Your mind is playing tricks on you. Why would a young girl want to shack up with a silly old goat like you? Don't you see that such a thing would be preposterous? Farcical? And why would she bring her baby up into the house? God, look at it...' The words on the baby monitor paused. After a few moments, Nigel resumed: 'Think about it, dad. I'm pleading here. Try to make *sense* of what is happening. You are being cheated. She's a faker.'

'She hasn't shacked up. She lives across the road...'

'Where is she then?'

'Er?'

'Is she across the road right now?'

'Erm, no, not really...'

'What a surprise — is she upstairs in your bed?'

'Of course not!'

'This situation needs to be fixed. I need to think things over. I need to organise power of attorney. That's the answer. It might be against your wishes, but your mental capacity has diminished alarmingly quickly. I guess a power of attorney, over you, will be my best option. You cannot take care of your own wellbeing and you're in danger of making serious financial gaffes, so I need to take control of the estate. For everyone's sake.'

'What do you mean, financial gaffes?'

'Did she bring the cot and bedclothes with her when she moved in?'

'No, she didn't need to because… Well, she hasn't…'

'No. Because you bought them for her, didn't you?'

'Yes but —'

'Exactly. You gave her a few quid, a few shillings, here and there. That's how these scammers operate. They connive the gullible out of a few measly quid to start with. Then they grow braver. Soon she will convince you to revise your will, and name her and the baby as beneficiaries. Then she'll get you to sign over the house and get you to transfer your savings to her.'

'Do not be ridiculous.'

'Ridiculous, is it? She's an old geezer squeezer. We find similar women all over the world. They seek-out lonely sad idiots like you. Do you honestly think she's interested in you? Of course she's *not*. She's drawn to your big fat house. Drawn to your big fat savings book. And drawn to your big fat pension.'

'She's not. What about the baby, though? What about her?'

'Bringing the child into your home is part of the coercion process. It's part of her scam. You are not thinking straight. These are her tactics…'

'But it's not. Won't you listen? The girl's innocent. And the baby is lost.'

'Think what you want. But anyone with half a healthy mind would know when they are being flattered and seduced. She's out to grab your life savings. I'm not going to let her get away with it…'

'That's what you're worried about, isn't it? Your birth-right?'

'It's only natural that a son should be concerned about his father's health and happiness. Especially if his father is entering waning years.'

'But honestly, it's about the money, isn't it? The house and deeds...'

'I won't be drawn on that right now. I will find a lawyer and get a legal solution. I am going to contact a general practitioner for you as well. See if we can drum a little sense into your befogged mind before it's too late. Meantime, do me a favour, will you? Get rid of the girl.'

The baby monitor goes dead.

Eimear distinguishes heavy footsteps travelling the hallway. She hears a clatter as the front door is closed. She thinks she hears sniffles. Then all goes silent. She waits a little while before going out to calm the poor old man. His nerves are shot to pieces.

They chomp open sandwiches together, and rest in enormous wing-chairs in chill light. George looks dispirited.

'The baby transmitter works well,' Eimear declares.

The old man arches a silver eyebrow. Then he crumples his nose and squeezes his brow: 'Oh me, oh my,' he says.

'I heard *everything*...'

'I'm sorry, Miss Yaymarr — you want to go leave us now?'

'No, I won't be going anywhere. We're making headway. Don't you think?'

'I cannot blame you for going. I cannot blame you for thinking it is not worth it.' The old man shrugs.

'The little girl and everything — I cannot leave her. I can't leave you to face things alone, either. It's a skawly mess you got yourself into, for sure. And your son thinks you're losing your noodle — but this is not your fault.'

'So what will you decide, Miss Yaymarr?'

'I have decided what I will do. I will move in.'

'Move in?'

'Well, sure, everybody thinks I moved in *anyways*. And it's only for a few days, isn't it? Until the situation is worked out, I mean. And my niminy landlady is making things unpleasant. So, would you mind if I moved in?'

'I *want* you to.'

'So you agree? Do you have a spare room for me to sleep?'

'You could use my daughter's room.'

'You never said you had a daughter. The first I heard about her was on the baby monitor.'

'Oh?'

'Where is she?'

'She lives in the Far East. With her husband. They have cats.'

'Does she have children?'

'Cats.'

'Do you have any other secrets, George?'

'What type?'

Eimear chuckles. 'What type? You *are* funny, George! I meant, are there any other mystery children you haven't told me about?'

'Only those two.'

'When did she move to the Far East?'

'Before my wife died, she couldn't even come back for the funeral.'

'Sorry.'

'My son will not be happy to find you're staying.'

'I don't give two squirts what that lank thinks.'

7

On Saturday, she collects meagre possessions and pushes them into a light duffel bag that her mother lent her before her trip from Éire.

Afterwards, Eimear dashes to George's place to let herself in. She calls for the old man and she hears a grizzled bleat coming from the main room, so guesses the old man is busy. Instead, she goes to locate her new bedroom, to stow her stuff. She finds a room that's fresh, although not very modern. It's pretty and female with girly backgrounds, soft shapes, and curved lines. There are cushions and pillows, plus romantic curtains. Eimear is happy with the atmosphere, so goes down to tell George how much she *loves* it.

She bursts into the living room and is surprised to see that he entertains a female guest. The guest sits on the same chair that Eimear *normally* occupies and is around about the same age too—maybe a couple of years older, but not much more.

This *new girl* has thin, oily hair, a tattered face and paunchy body-shape.

'Hello Miss Yaymarr...' says George. 'I'll introduce you to Arnie.'

'Arnie?'

'Hi,' says the girl. She rises. 'I know it sounds like a boy's name. Mad, isn't it? My parents were adventurous when they christened me...' The new girl gives Eimear a hearty smile and then stretches out pudgy fingers for a moist handshake.

George lifts his old bones from the armchair and says, 'She's my son's girlfriend. I'll leave you to get acquainted.'

'OK, so.'

'It's nice to meet you,' Arnie says. 'I've heard *everything* about you. From Nigel.'

'I expect he sent you over to see what's happening...' Eimear suggests.

George leaves the room. Once he's gone, they sit. Arnie continues: 'No, I came of own free will...Though I can't deny Nigel's been less than complimentary about you. It's clear he doesn't accept your presence in the family home. When he came back to our place, he blathered wildly about you *stealing* his father's things. I thought I'd better come and see for myself. Try to find the underlying cause of his concern... but I aim to be reasonable and level-headed.'

'I haven't stolen his father's things. You can report back.'

'I'm sure you haven't. But he's worried you've inserted yourself into the old man's life. He thinks you're doing a bit of sugar-daddying.'

'Right so. And might I also be trying to grab a share of his inheritance? '

'I'm sure we can be friends, can't we? Whatever the situation is, I'm sure we can be like adults, yes? I just wanted to come over and chat, girl-to-girl, like. You don't mind, do you?'

'Not at all.' Eimear but slides her adjacent chair askew so she can examine Arnie's eyes and watch the body-language. 'So tell me,' she says, 'How long have you been with Nigel?'

'Five years.'

'Wow! That's a long time. Living together?'

'Since his mother died.'

'Do you have children?'

'Er, no. We have a boxer dog.'

'Of course. George takes care of the dog while your husband goes to the gym.'

'We're not married.'

'No? A married type relationship though? Didn't you want to go through with a ceremony?'

'I did! I very much wanted a ceremony. But Nigel is a commit-ment-phobe. We have been together all this time and he never once popped the question.'

'Ouch.'

'But he's a good guy. Regular job. Takes care of himself. Good with his hands, around the home, I mean ...'

'How did you meet?'

'He set-up the air conditioning in our office. That's what he does. He's a heating and air-conditioning engineer. I work in a call centre in town. One day I saw him up a ladder flexing his muscles and I thought, like a girl does, I'd like that man to exert his muscles on me, right? So, the rest is history.'

Eimear screwed up her brows: 'Do you mind me saying some-thing? There's quite a big age difference between you and Nigel, isn't there?'

'Yes, that's right... A couple of my friends also commented. But I tell you the truth, I never think about it. I mean, he is...' Arnie bends her head low to say the next bit quietly: 'I've been his first woman... I mean I was his first woman, you know, the first woman he'd ever been in bed with, so to speak... I mean, I was his *first* when I met him.'

'Gosh.'

'Yes, I know. Over forty and inactive. Amazing, huh? Like the movie with Steve Carell.'

'I never saw the movie...'

'Anyway — he was inexperienced when I met him, and I think he's still quite childlike and innocent. I think until he knew me, he had only loved his own company. He lived a very private life — he and his father. No one else came into it. They played with models. Went for long walks. Talked about projects...'

'Do you think they're alike? George and Nigel?'

'There must be similarities, of course. Dad is systematic. His son, *less so...*'

'I think the appearance of the baby has upset George...' Eimear comments. "His organized routine is ruined...'

'Yes, the baby. I wanted to talk about that...'

'Mmm?'

'Nigel thinks the baby is *yours*.'

'Have you seen her?'

'She's a delightful little thing. You must be immensely proud.'

'Seen the skin?'

'It's brown. I understand that. What matters these days is that you love one another and love your baby. Skin colour is of no importance. Not these says. The world's a great big melting pot.'

'She's not mine.'

'Nigel told me you might say that. So what's the story?'

'Didn't George tell you about the baby?'

'He says something about finding the child on a beach. But the story sounds far-fetched. Nigel says his father is covering *for you*.'

'Well, actually the baby has nothing to do with me! Nothing at all. George found her on the beach. He brought her home in a bucket. Imagine that? That's when I came over to help.'

'Seems odd.'

'Uh-huh.'

'And police and social services — what do they say about this? Have you reported it?'

'Yes, we have...' Arnie gives a little gulp as if she didn't expect *that* reply. 'The police are dragging their feet.'

'And you? You and George *I mean*. Are you and George... sorry to press this... but are you an item? I'm sorry if the question is direct, but it is what Nigel thinks.'

Eimear splutters, 'We are *not* romantically involved, if that is what you are suggesting. Actually, I find the proposal pretty nauseating.'

'Sorry.'

'No, it's fine. It's probably best to get things get cleared up.'

'But you've been hanging together a lot, haven't you? Lately I mean. And you moved yourself into his place. Don't you think it might get serious between you and George?'

'Did George tell you I moved in?'

'No — Nigel did.'

'Well, that's funny because how did he know? But, yes, it's true, I moved in. But *literally* just ten minutes ago. And only for the time being. And only while I help care for the child. And only until she's returned safely to her parents. Then, once the baby is back with her mum, I'll go to my digs. I will probably never speak to George once this episode is over.'

'That's a shame.'

'Is it?'

'I guess you're probing me — you're playing devil's advocate? I don't blame you for trying. So, here's the truth: I came to help George because he's an old man who found himself in a difficult situation that is *way* beyond him. I'm not getting a single penny out of the arrangement. I haven't misled or deceived *anyone*. And it's *not* a relationship — I'm just being *neighbourly*, that's all. I just want to be sure the child is safely delivered back to someone who loves her. That's all there is to this.'

'I see.'

8

At Saturday lunchtime a stylish woman arrives at George's door. They see her arrive through the net curtains. The woman is dressed in a coral hat, with white gloves and a shiny blue handbag. There is a row of pearls around the loose flab of her neck. She'd dressed as if she's about to go to the Queen's races. The woman looks about forty, with a face that has been routinely — and probably cheaply — aggrandized by Superdrug's *own-brand* cosmetics.

The door-bell rings. Eimear answers it.

'Hello young lady. I'm calling for Mister Florn. Is he in?'

'What's this in connection with?'

'It's a local council matter...'

'OK, then. You'd better come in.'

Eimear opens the door wide, and the woman enters. She wipes her heels on their coconut door matting. She has good manners, so waits by the telephone table. 'Where is the old gentleman?' she enquires.

'I'll call for him,' Eimear says. 'He's in the workshop... *George, it's the council here.* They want to see you...'

The woman offers Eimear a graceful smile. There's no scurrying sound from the rear, so Eimear gestures along the hallway, 'Do you want to go into the living room, Missus? To take the strain off your pins? Sit down, I'll go get him.'

'Can I see the baby before?'

'OK, so. The tiny one is along this way; do you want to follow me? She's laid in the back room.'

Eimear leads the woman to baby Amira. The child is absorbed in sweet dreams.

'As I thought...' says the council lady. She gazes into the cot.

'As you thought, what?'

'I'll discuss it with the elderly gentleman if you don't mind.'

'Oh? Very well then. This way.'

George finally makes his way from the workshop and enters the main room. He wipes his hands on a paper napkin as he comes in.

'It's the lady from the council...' announces Eimear.

George gives the woman a peculiar look — his eyebrows undulating. He extends a dusty hand for the woman to shake. She declines. 'I'm Mrs Anne Hanson-Bhatia...' she declares. 'I'm the elected councillor for a neighbouring ward. I'm here to resolve a *problem*...'

'Problem?' says George.

'I'm here to follow-up on a report made by one of my voting residents. I hope you won't mind if I ask you a couple of questions...'

'Are you not from the social services?' asks Eimear.

'I'm a councillor,' says the woman, offering a pencil-thin smile through sticky lips.

'But not from social services? Only — we are waiting for social services to respond about the baby. I thought that's why you were here. It's why I showed you the infant...'

'Oh, I'm sure they will respond, *now*. Once I've played my part in this business. Now I've seen the child for myself, and I add weight to the difficult situation we find ourselves in, we'll get things expedited, I'm sure.'

'What *situation* is that?' George asks.

'About the migrant child and so on...' continues the council lady.

'Migrant?'

'A local resident notified me that you are secretly harbouring an illegal alien here — *sheltering* is the valid word— you are *sheltering* a non-native baby at this address. Is their report accurate?'

'No.'

'But I've seen the child myself, haven't I? And the skin is certainly brown.'

'Do what?' Eimear asks. She crosses her arms over her chest.

'So where are the parents, might I ask ? Have they have paid you to foster this illegal alien? If so, what were the arrangements?'

'We're tending for the little *babby* until her mummy can be located...' Eimear explains.

'What if this *so-called* mother can't be found?' Mrs Hanson-Bhatia asks. 'What happens next? No doubt you'll be bringing the child up as your own. As a naturalized citizen? Yes? Perhaps, miraculously, her parents will appear a year or so down the line. Of course, they'll be granted asylum, won't they? You'll be well rewarded too, won't you, once the baby is handed over? That's the plan, isn't it? Collect the cash?'

'What is all this?' Eimear asks.

'It's balderdash...' George adds.

'I'll take a few notes while I'm here,' continues Mrs Hanson-Bhatia. 'So I can inform the authorities.' She takes a gilded notebook from her bag.

'Where are you from?' George asks.

'Like I already told you— I'm the elected councillor of an adjacent neighbourhood.'

'Are *you* my councillor?'

'Yes and no. Strictly speaking, I am *not*. But I'm an elected representative of your neighbour.'

'So you are *not* my representative?' asks George.

'Not strictly speaking. But I'm here to speak on behalf of the wider community. A community that is concerned about what is going on here.'

'Who's concerned, exactly? We've been trying to get help for days... nobody has been listening,' Eimear suggests.

'It would not be fair to reveal which of your fellow citizens has raised concerns. I promised I'd look into things.'

'It's that old bat from across the way...' Eimear claims.

'No it's not...' George tells her. 'She lives in the same ward as us. It must be someone who lives beyond the church on the hill.'

The woman opens her notebook. 'Some information then...' she draws up a fancy pen and clicks it.

'Do you have an identity card— or a badge to prove who you are?' Eimear asks.

'Like I told you, young lady, I'm not from the social services. I'm a local politician. We don't need to carry identity cards.' The woman issues a pint-size laugh at such a ridiculous suggestion.

'In that case you can leave,' George says.

'But I've only just come.'

'You're not welcome. I'll see you to the door.'

'Well, *really*...'

They accompany Mrs Hanson-Bhatia to the hallway where she gives Eimear a look of derision: 'You should be ashamed of yourself...' the woman says, 'With a man three times your age! You are nothing but a fizz-gigging little minx...'

'How dare you!' shouts Eimear.

'And *you* —' Mrs Hanson-Bhatia turns to George. 'Hmph! You're worse. You are a doddery half-witted old lecher with a love for brown skin...'

'Get out.'

They watch the woman trot along their front path.

'What a repugnant chunk of imperiousness...' offers George.

'Agreed,' says Eimear.

A little while later, Eimear searches Google on her smartphone. 'Anne Hanson-Bhatia. Councillor. Putting England First,' she reads. 'Making England great again. *Well, I never...*'

'I thought I recognized her repulsive face...' George says.

'I'm sorry I let the racist in, George. Surely, I am. I genuinely thought she was from the social services...'

'No yarm done.'

They bring baby Amira to the central police station on Sunday. They walk because it's not far, and the weather is reasonable. Along the way, Eimear becomes concerned about the prospering size of the baby. She's already too big for their carry-sling.

'We should indeed have a push-chair by now,' comments Eimear. 'The infant has doubled in size, just in one week! Sure, this contraption won't last another six days.' Eimear keeps her hands under the weight of the baby to offer extra security and she feels the roll and pitch of the baby's warm bottom beneath her forearms.

'Do you want me to take the baby?'

'No, George, you're right.'

'Don't you ever get a night off duty, Miss Yaymarr?'

'Not really, so.'

'How does it work? Are you required to work every night?'

'Pretty much. On the contract they have me on *anyways*. Some girls are on zero-hours. I'm lucky. Zero hours is much worse. Those girls stay at home, they have no money, and they must wait for a call. If a call comes, they rush in. I'm one of the fortunate ones.'

The old man's eyebrows twist and groove, 'It does not sound right,' he grumbles.

'If I wanted, I could request a day of leave. It's allowed in my contract. I have to apply in advance, though. And it might not be permitted. It would cost me a day's wages, *too*. Do you have anything in mind? Something that's worth taking a day's unpaid leave?'

'We need to go to London soon, that's all. Investigating.'

'Is this connected to your theory about her falling from a boat?'

George nods: 'Jersey Island said a craft headed into mixed tides...'

'You go if you want... I'll stay here to take care of the little one. As long as you're back by six, I can get to work. '

They arrive at the police station. The bottom entrance is fixed and bolted. There's no one is at home. 'Maybe it's closed on Sunday,' suggests Eimear. They climb the concrete stairs to get up to the main door of the station, which is tough to reach. It's a long climb for George. A notice on *this door* states 'The station is open 10am to 6pm MON-FRI. In an emergency phone 999.'

They stumble down the dangerous stairs, then peer through bars on the side of the building, and into the courtyard. They see rows-upon-rows of parked police cars. There's not a soul about.

'This is madness,' says Eimear. We did all this. We walked all the way to the major station. And to find that it's closed. Madness. Where are all Peelers?'

'What's happened to this country?' George asks.

They start their long hike home.

At teatime, baby Amira pulls herself onto tiny feet and grabs the cushion from the armchair. She provides a satisfied smile when it falls down.

'She's going from strength-to-strength,' Eimear observes. 'If we have to keep her any longer, we'll need a play-pen, a baby walker and a push-chair.'

'She said words yesterday, too. She might say them again...'

'What words? I hope you did not teach her to say mum. Please, I could not bear it. '

'I was teaching her to say the word *potty* for me.'

'Potty? She hasn't got one. What were you thinking? Why did you get her to say that?'

'I thought she might try —'

Eimear interrupts: 'We need to get her a cuddly toy. Poor thing. She has nothing to interact with...'

George keenly scrutinises the baby, then rushes away. A little later, he returns with a dusty rag-doll. He passes it to Eimear so she can check-it before delivering it to the child.

'My daughter's...' George explains. 'It was her favourite doll, so I kept it.'

The baby takes the doll with a huge smile, then drops it. She bumps onto her bottom and crawls after the toy.

'You don't talk much about your daughter...' Eimear says. 'Why is that?'

'I don't have much to say. Though I miss her.'

On Monday morning Eimear foregoes sleep because they must take baby Amira to the developmental clinic.

At the major hospital, they see a paediatrician who checks the child's eyesight, hearing, motor co-ordination, attention span and concentration.

'I don't think there's any need for a formal assessment...' the doctor tells them. 'But I can arrange for an outreach visit if you'd like.'

'We're fine...' Eimear remarks because, above all, she wants to go home and sleep.

So they take a Big Red Taxi back to the house.

Once indoors, George takes the child for a nappy change.

Eimear stretches and yawns in the front room and, as she does, she sees a woman parading their front path. It looks like Mrs. Slaviaro — the proprietor of the housing opposite.

Eimear goes to the hall and throws open the front door to greet her landlady. Mrs. Slaviaro has an unbuttoned house-coat stretched over gloomy shoulders. She looks like she's in a hurry.

'Howya, missus, how can I help?' Eimear asks.

'I'm glad I caught you...' says Mrs. Slaviaro. 'I want to give you this. They say I need to deliver it directly.' Her proprietor passes a thick letter. 'It's a notice to quit.'

'Quit?'

'Well, you're not there, are you? So what does it matter?'

'I would like to come back, though. *Here* is only temporary. *This* is only a stopgap arrangement...'

'Well, you should have thought about that before you jumped into bed with *him*, shouldn't you?'

'What's that supposed to mean?'

'Look, this neighbourhood has standards. Specific standards of decorum and other general *what-not*. They notified me your conduct violates common codes of decency. Your moral turpitude breaches common guidelines *and so on*... it's all there, writ down plain, in the letter.'

'Are you allowed to evict me? Is it lawful? I haven't done any damage or violated any of your rules! My rent payments have been on time...'

'You haven't violated none of the rules? Really? That's a hoot! What about migrant smuggling? What about false testimony? What about depraved catholic practices? What about general Irish wickedness?'

'I believe those things are in your head.'

'In my head, are they? What a nerve you've got, my girl. And it's not even me complaining. It's the neighbours. I should have listened to them. *Don't take an Irish,* they told me. *The Irish is dirty and foul,* they said. *I'm a Christian,* I told them, I will let one under my roof if that's what I want to do. *You'll be sorry,* they told me. What happened? What did I beget for all my trouble?'

'I don't know. I don't even understand what *beget* means.'

'I've been criticised by my fellow citizens... that's what holy charity has beggeted me. You *shouldn't let her* into our community, they advised. She'll *conduct wicked ways* from your rooms, they declared. *Irish are black,* they whispered. You shouldn't facilitate *unseemly behaviour*, they insisted. And this is what my Christian heart has begotten unto me.'

'I see.'

'So, this is a formal notice to quit. I will re-let your room in fourteen days. Don't come back. My next tenant will be a nice white English girl. With morals. Someone I can be proud of.'

The following morning, upon returning from a busy shift at Clongowes House, Eimear sees a strange car parked outside the old man's house. The motor is burnished, like the skin of a tansy drisheen. It is fitted with smoky windows and chrome accessories. It reminds Eimear of the vehicle they sent to collect her maimeó's cold body.

'Oh, Jesus and Mary what is this then?' she whispers. She pads down the red tiled path to the front door and feels a dull ache on her insides. She's aware that a side door on the undertaker's vehicle slides back. She picks up a male voice, 'Good morning to you,' the voice shouts.

She turns, to face it: 'Can I help?'

'I'm here to visit Mister Florn... But he hasn't been out to answer his door yet...'

'It's too early...'

'I'm told he rises with the birds and takes regular exercises on the vestibule...'

'That is usually true,' she explains. 'But things are frenzied these days. His routine has been disturbed.'

'That's what I wanted to talk to him about. His demanding schedule.'

'And who would you be when you're at home?'

'Me miss? I'm with the County Echo. My name is Pinsmail. Lawton Pinsmail.' He announces himself as if he's a secret agent.

'Go away.'

'What was that?'

'You don't say...'

Eimear is aware that another figure lingers inside the gloomy van. This shadowy figure points a long lens her way.

Pinsmail extends his legs and approaches. He stops at the garden gate. His platinum hair is spiked high with gel and his cheap suit gleams optimistically in the morning light. She distinguishes Superdrug own-brand aftershave at twenty paces. 'Maybe I can talk to *you*...' says the man.

'I don't think so.'

'Oh, please. I've waited here so long. I want to be your first.'

'First what?'

'First to get a handle.'

'What do you mean?'

'News and so on. Human interest. We want to get a local story before the networks.'

'I think you must have the wrong place.'

'Doesn't George Florn live here?'

'He does, but —'

'Right place then.'

She senses movement from inside the van and hears a series of motorized clicks.

'We do not have the facts — just what's been spread by the Mudgekicker,' he continues.

'What's the Mudgekicker?'

'It's a woman. Don't you have Twitter?'

'Not really,' she says. 'I must be getting inside. I ask you to leave. I need to get myself indoors. I'm tired after night-shift.' Eimear reaches for her keys and turns her back on the man.

'She does gigantic campaigns on Twitter,' he continues. 'Mudge-kicker is huge on social media, thousands of followers.'

Eimear turns again. 'What's this got to do with the old man? Someone has been codding you, I daresay. I think you might be foost-ering a good time here.'

'Mudgekicker is putting together a story.'

'About Mister Florn?'

'It's going to be a shitstorm...'

'That's not a pleasant expression, sir. We don't like vulgarity in this neighbourhood. There's a baby indoors. You know he's an elderly man, don't you? We don't require intrusion and vulgar words...'

'Well it's a good job I'm here. So I can help clear things. Get things sewn tight. Sort wheat from chaff. I can do lots of good before things go mad and distortion sets in. That's why I'm here *early* — to cover things before it goes viral.'

'Viral? What does that mean? I don't know what any of this means. What has all this got to do with us?'

'Can I get in and question Mister Florn?'

'No, you certainly *cannot*.'

The man falters by the front gate. It seems he can't pass over their threshold without permission. He's, basically, a modern-day vampire. 'Just a quick chat and snapshot, please?' he begs.

Eimear jiggles her key in the lock and wrenches open the front door. She hears several clicks from the van as she enters. She pushes the door shut and listens from inside.

'Shit... *storm-aah...*' shouts Pinsmail, from the safety of the kerb.

Eimear arrives early for duty at Clongowes House.

Mrs Soomro, who manages the residential home during night hours, is waiting. She invites Eimear to come for a chat before the evening tasks begin.

'Do you want to see missus?' asks Eimear.

'Your affairs are a private matter. I don't want to intrude...'

'OK, so...'

'But there's a man to see you.'

'A man?'

'I put him in the guest lounge.'

'Who is it?'

'How should I know? I thought you'd be able to tell me! Your private matters are best kept private, dear, but I warn you *not* to invite anyone here again. It's your job at stake.'

'I did not invite anyone.'

'Well, he says that you *did*. He says he's here to discuss a personal matter.'

'I better see him.'

'Well, don't be long. Things are hectic. See him quick and tell him to leave. We don't require distractions.'

'Yeah sure, missus...'

'And Eimear...'

'Yup?'

'Do not let this happen again.'

'Right so.'

Eimear approaches the glass entrance of the guest lounge. She glowers through the gap in the door. She sees a spruce man togged in a semi-stylish suit. She recognises his fussy hair — it's Lawton Pins-mail, the guy from earlier. The Echo journalist. She pushes the door to enter the lounge and face him. She prepares a distorted pout. 'Why you here?' she shouts. 'You need to *get out* this instant.'

The young man offers an adequate smile.

Eimear puts her arms on her hips and tilts her head, waiting for a response. The guy stands motionless. He doesn't lose his cool. His mouth opens, but no words come out.

'Why are you here?' she repeats. Her voice getting louder.

'Miss Lambe, I have been waiting to talk to you —'

'Why have you come to my workplace? How did you get my details? You've landed me in big trouble...'

'I need to see you. I got info from your landlady...'

There's a long pause: 'You have no right to poke your nose into my business.'

'I have *every* right. It's what I do.'

'Do you? Well, it's not a dignified occupation, is it?'

'Sorry, do you mind if I sit? I've been at it for hours. Getting worn, standing...' Pinsmail points to his feet.

'At it for hours, eh? Sniffing, digging, and prodding. It must be genuinely hard for you... you snooping rat.'

Eimear pushes the door shut. She slams her backside into a beige leather lounge-chair. He comes to sit near. He sighs. The long exhalation gives her an extra moment to consider his sinewy body and biggish feet.

'Did you tell the old man about the shitstorm?' he asks.

She shakes her head.

'Don't you think he'd understand?'

'Of course he *wouldn't*... he's over eighty for heaven's sake. Get real.' Eimear rubs an imperceptible mark from her cheeks. 'Are you some kind of imbecile?'

The guy gives half a shrug, then leans forward. 'If you tell me your story, it might help get rid of *others*.'

'What others?' she mumbles.

'The shitstorm is coming.'

She examines her nails and finds flakes around the cuticles. She hears Pinsmail fidgeting with a pen. She looks over, 'What is there to say?' Her mind wanders over the last few days. 'There was a baby on a beach. I went to help an old man. We waited; we're still waiting, for the authorities to do *something*. Hopefully, the parents will arrive soon. To take the baby back. Then I can return to my regular life.'

'And?'

'And *nothing*. Some council-woman visited. She saw the child...'

'Ah, yes. Councillor Hanson-Bhatia.'

'Is she your informant?'

'Not mine.' Pinsmail runs fingers through over-gelled hair. 'Awful woman, I can't stand her...'

'If she isn't dishing the dirt, who is?'

'I will not reveal my source, of course.'

'Right, so.'

'But the Mudgekicker — the woman on Twitter — she seems to think he's *done this before*.'

'Who has?'

'The old man.'

'You what?' Eimear's posture stiffens. She shakes her head.

'That's the story, anyway. Didn't you know? Maybe it's true. Maybe it's *not*. I shouldn't have said anything. Your reaction proves that you didn't know.'

'Are you suggesting this is the second baby the old man found on a beach?'

Pinsmail tilts his head back and sniggers, 'I'm *not* saying that...'

'What are you saying, then?'

'Maybe I shouldn't have mentioned it.'

'Well, you *did* —now you should expand on it...' Eimear frowns.

'The locals tell me he was suspected of bringing refugees to England. That's back in the day.'

'When was this?'

'Oh, I don't know for sure... according to your landlady, thirty years ago. Maybe more.'

'Please confirm, I pray. Please tell me he didn't find a baby on a beach back then?'

'I don't know.'

'You don't know, or you won't say?'

'Really, *I don't know.* Maybe I should leave it. I don't want anyone to get into trouble. I'm just trying to cover a human-interest story... I'm trying to find an angle.'

'Oh God, Jesus...'

'What is he like? The old man? Got his head screwed on? Not soft in the bonce, is he?'

'I don't think so. He's lonely. He makes small models in his workshop. He prefers routine.'

The reporter watches her face and prepares his next question: 'Why did you move in with him?'

'I'm way over my head...' she whispers.

'Your landlady has a distorted vision of you. She says you have twisted the old man around your finger. She says you're out to snatch his *mullah*. She suggests you are money-grabbing...'

'I went to help. Honest.'

'Your landlady doesn't seem to like you.'

'Irish?'

'That's the main reason...'

'What is wrong with everybody? Why won't they leave us alone?'

'People like Councillor Hanson-Bhatia and your landlady are in charge of things these days. Nauseous shits like the Mudgekicker get them *worked up*. The haters gain prestige, the victims grow weaker. These days it's the loudmouths who dominate our agenda. We must get used to it, because the loudmouths are here to stay...'

'Is this why the story is getting attention?'

'Today's newspaper is tomorrow's chip paper... you know that. But the moment 'uncontrolled immigration' is used in a headline, it becomes a rallying call for the idiots who say the State ignored them for too long. Petty-minded bigots. They slithered out from their shit-heaps while the rest of us forgot to pay them any attention. These same shits find allies on social networks... allies who agree with their warped views and share vile opinions. So, now, they think they can say what they bloody-well like.'

'How can I help?'

'Just tell your story. It's all you can do.'

'What about the old man?'

'It's up to him — he can do whatever he wants.'

'And the baby?'

'God knows what becomes of the child. Tell me the truth... is she yours?'

'No, of course she's *not*. The old man found her. He found her on the beach.'

'You'd better tell me all you know.'

Ten minutes later, Mrs. Soomro watches the journalist leave the building. She has stern eyes.

Once he's safely out of sight, the manager locks the place down and turns to Eimear, 'Not again. No other visitors.'

'Right you are, missus,' says Eimear.

When Eimear arrives home after night-shift, she finds a crowd of boisterous journalists waiting for the old man to surface. They remind her of a gaggle of rough geese she once saw on the Wexford Slobs.

'Where is the migrant from?' honks one.

'When will the child be repatriated?' cries another.

She spies councillor Hanson-Bhatia in the group. She is also shouting her mouth off: 'Send all migrants home. There's no room for them. England for the English,' she squawks.

Eimear puts her hands over her cheeks to protect her face from camera-shot. She pushes up the garden path.

'Does the Home Office know about this? What about the Immigration Service?' shouts a man in the street, holding a microphone.

She enters the house and pushes the door closed with her backside. George stands in the hallway. The old man faces her.

'They have been massing since the early hours of morn...' he murmurs.

'I've got a bone to pick with you...' she replies.

'What?'

She leans on the door because she can't decide whether to stop or go. She takes three full breaths before she is able to continue: 'Tell me the truth, George.'

'What about?'

'Did you do *all this* before?'

'Did I do what?'

'Did you find a child on the beach? Are you a repeat offender?'

'What do you mean?'

'Tell me...' she presses her fingers into his chest. Her chin quivers.

'Why are all those people here?' the old man mumbles.

'Don't you know George? Are you *honestly* saying you don't know?'

George straightens his spine and tucks his arms by his sides. 'What are you on about, Miss?'

'Is this the first child you have ever found?'

'Obviously, it is.'

'Why do people say you did this before?'

'Did what?'

'Are you telling the truth, George?'

'I have no idea what this is about. I do not know what you mean.'

Eimear takes a deep breath, 'I need to think...'

'Are you going? Will you not stay and help?'

She shakes her head to avoid eye-contact with him. Then, using a soft voice, barely a breath, she says: 'I've got no place else to go...'

George gazes at her greasy hair and then runs an old finger across her wrinkled, discouraged brow: 'You'd better sleep, Miss. I'll deal with things. You seem mixed-up.'

'Maybe.' Eimear pushes beyond the old man to get to the kitchen. She wants a glass of water before bed. 'You must *not* mislead me, George. Never! God help me if I find you've deceived me, George. Because I will throttle your scruffy neck if I find you've lied to me... Do you hear?'

His feet fidget. The old man fiddles with his shirt sleeves.

'I have a bad feeling in my belly about all this. I'm thinking you're up to no good. Well? Are you legit George?"

'Of course I yam...'

'I don't know if you've been entirely truthful with me... tell me now, have you?'

The old man tightens the bony ridge above his eyes. 'I did everything with good intentions, believe me,' he says.

'Right then.'

In the afternoon George's son comes over, unannounced, with his girlfriend, Arnie.

Eimear opens the door to them. 'You're still here,' Nigel says with a sniff. Eimear checks the front garden as she closes the door, to confirm, at least in her own mind, that the gaggle of reporters had departed.

She leads the visitors into the living room. Arnie fabricates a temporary smile. She sits on the biggest armchair.

Nigel stands. 'Where's pop?' he asks. His eyes wander around the room. It's as if he seeks to figure out if anything has changed, altered, or had been stolen (by her) since his last visit.

'He's washing his hands. He fed the baby. He'll be in shortly,' Eimear explains

Arnie's eyes brighten: 'And how is baby? Is she well?'

'Oh yes,' Eimear answers.

A little later the old man enters. He smiles at Arnie then studies his son.

'I'm sorry Dad...' Nigel says.

"I'm sorry *too*.'

'You first then...'

'Well, I yam sorry I did not include you from the beginning.' Nigel nods. George continues: 'I should have told you right away about the baby. I yam sorry I did not look after your dog. It was busy here, and I did not think it would be nice to have a canine around the house with a young-un on the floor...'

'The dog has *gone*...'

'What?'

Eimear jerks her head back. She bends her neck to observe Nigel's face.

'She made me do it...' accuses Nigel. He has a clenched jaw. Eimear supposes he means *her*, for some reason, but then she recognizes that he's looking at Arnie.

Arnie pinches the bridge of her nose before explaining: 'If I'm honest, I think the dog was a step too far for us. A step too far as a couple, I mean. We didn't have time, you see, and we didn't have energy... for a dog. It takes a lot of stamina, and we couldn't handle it, neither physically nor mentally. Nigel goes to the gym every afternoon. I lounge on the sofa when I get home from work. It takes a great deal of effort to keep a dog. We didn't have time for all those walks.'

'Gosh! What happened to your puppy?' Eimear asks.

'We found a new home for him. A suitable home. We're not sad. It was a good move.'

'I yam sorry to hear that,' adds the old man says. 'Perhaps I should have helped y'out more, I don't know.'

'Oh well,' Nigel says. His shoulders slump. 'One of those things I suppose.'

The air is fresh. An interlude elapses that allows everyone to contemplate all that has been said. Eimear is astonished to see that George and Nigel stand facing each other. Though neither budges an inch. It's as if they're play-acting the *roles* of father and son. She is sure there is of silent battle of wills going on, with neither willing to retreat or lose advantage, yet eager to make up.

The old man breaks the stalemate. He delivers a million-dollar question: 'What are *you* sorry for, son? What do you most regret?

'Me?'

'Hmhmm...'

'Er — *her* I suppose...'

'Miss Yaymaar?'

'Yeah, her and everything.'

'What about her?'

'Well, maybe I was wrong to suppose she's a gold-digger,' Nigel looks to Arnie for support. His girlfriend pushes strands of hair from her face and gives an encouraging glance that suggests he ought to continue. 'Er, she is um — well, she is here to help, isn't she? I suppose. And she is not what I thought she probably was. Maybe it wasn't the money game she has been playing. When I first met her, I thought she was an opportunist, you know what I mean?'

Eimear notices that Nigel doesn't look her way when he says all these things. It's as if he doesn't entirely believe them! She reckons he's going through the motions. As if he's reading from a script! He doesn't believe the words.

George steps closer to Nigel. For a moment, it appears they might embrace. Eimear secretly urges them to hug. But they *don't*. Instead, George offers a hand of reconciliation. His son takes the old man's hand and gives it a shake. There is no love between them. They function more like business partners.

'Can we see the baby?' asks Arnie. She directs these words at Eimear.

'Or is she sleeping?' says Nigel.

'Of course you can see her. You know where she is. The baby is in the back room. After lunch, she might be a little dozy. Since you last saw her, Nigel, she has grown a lot. She crawls everywhere. George taught her some new words and she can stand with support. If we keep her any longer, we'll need a walker...'

'It's another thing I wanted to talk to you about, dad,' Nigel says. 'I wonder how long you will keep her. Only, I know it can't be easy for you. And what happens next? What should you do, according to experts? I mean, you've only got temporary custody, haven't you? When will her guardianship be sorted out?'

'We're waiting to return the young one to her rightful parents,' says George.

'Not likely to happen though, is it?'

'Why not?'

'Well, you know., the circumstances of her discovery and all that. Er? And the fact you have been, you know, er, you have been *concealing* her —'

Eimear butts in: 'We haven't concealed her! Why would you say such a thing?'

'Why aren't the police involved?'

'They are involved! It's just that they seem to drag their feet.'

Nigel gives a tight smile. 'Have you notified them? Officially. I don't think that you have...'

'We reported her as soon as we found her. Right away. Didn't we?' Eimear turns to George for reassurance. 'We submitted a police report right away.'

'Anyway...'

'I think what Nigel is saying,' interrupts Arnie. 'Is that this case should be handed to the social services. You should get them started on the process of fostering. So this babe can be looked after *accordingly*.'

'We told them,' Eimear adds. 'They're waiting for the police to do their end of things. I don't know why it's so complex or why it takes so long — but it does.'

'Actually, I have great faith the parents will take her,' George remarks.

'Do you?' says Nigel. 'It seems a dose *unlikely* to me.'

'Why?'

'It's already taken too long, hasn't it? They'd have been here by now, wouldn't they? I think her true parents are gone. I think they've vanished'

There's another long hush while everyone reflects on what's been aired. Eimear jumps in: 'Well, you say you want to see the baby. Why don't you do that now?'

Arnie sits up. She bounces her knees. 'Ooh yes.'

'Well, go ahead. See the baby while your father and I make a pot of tea. A plate of sandwiches and a nice cup for everyone?'

'That would be nice.'

George gives Eimear a pained look as she drags him towards the kitchen. Meanwhile, Nigel and Arnie go to visit the baby in the back room.

Once they're out of earshot, Eimear diverts the old man towards the workshop and deftly closes the door. 'I thought we was off to make tea?' George grumbles.

'Shush!' Eimear puts a finger to the old man's lips and gestures him toward the 'listening end' of their baby monitor. The device sits under his workbench. She pushes him onto a stool, to make him comfortable, but essentially to stop him from shuffling about.

They hear 'coo-coo' noises coming from the loudspeaker. They distinguish Nigel's voice coming from the monitor: 'I don't know if we ought to get involved. This doesn't seem right...'

'Don't start all over,' they hear Arnie's voice say. 'I thought we previously discussed things...'

'It's a complicated business. And what about her? She'll get in the way, won't she?'

'She'll not be in our way. Anyway, I can handle her...'

'Really? What makes you think you can handle her?'

'She only came to help your dad, after all. I know you think she's meddling, but she's not...'

'That's your opinion...'

'And this is our best chance...'

'Even so.'

'You know we've been having issues. You know you're not getting younger. You know you can't...' Arnie's voice trails away. Then comes back louder: 'The doctor told you. And there are my bits too...'

They hear the baby gurgle over the speaker. George puckers his lips, and his eyebrows go hyperactive.

'How long do you believe it will take?' asks Nigel.

'She's lovely, isn't she? So sweet...'

'Yeah, great. Will social services allow it? '

'Yes, obviously. We offer a safe home, plus we already know the child. So we are the natural choice. Far better than staying here with a crazy old man.'

'Don't say my old man is crazy. He's eccentric, I grant you. But he's not crazy.' Nigel pauses. 'For me, it's the little madam he installed... she's the fly in the ointment. I judge it wise to get the baby away from her.'

'It's best you keep your thoughts to yourself... We don't want anyone getting distraught,' Arnie suggests. 'We'll get onto social services in the morning and start the ball rolling, huh? Why not remove the baby from the cot? Grab her up and give her a big hug.'

'No, I'd rather not — if it's all the same to you...'

'You will need to demonstrate you are a good parent with social services... You'll need to show affection *eventually*...'

'Later, then.'

'Shhh!'

Eimear pinches her head around the corner of the door and shouts *boo!* while the couple stand by the baby's cot.

The sudden noise makes Arnie jump. She produces an odd squawk. Nigel pinches her arm: '*Frick me...* you gave us both a terrible scare,' he shouts.

'Sorry,' says Eimear. 'I didn't mean to surprise you. You were deep in thought. I thought I'd come to see how you were getting on with baby. George is making the tea, so I told him I'd come and get you. Hasn't she grown?'

'Hmm...'

'Nigel?'

'Oh yeah, the baby. It cries, it poos, it pees, it sleeps, it eats, and it dribbles. Much the same as any other baby...'

'Don't you like babies?' Eimear asks. 'Why not take her up and give her a hug?'

'I won't if it's all the same,' Nigel says.

'You *should*...' Arnie hints.

'Why all this pressure?' he snaps. 'What's this shit? Why are you both ganging up on me?' Nigel makes a choking noise.

'We're not *ganging up*, honey-badger. It's just...'

'I'll leave it if you don't mind. God... I *already said*.' Nigel squeezes past the girls and skulks towards the living room. The girls are left behind with the baby. Eimear takes the infant from the cot and passes her to Arnie for a long hug. Arnie raises her eyebrows, and smiles as she takes the baby. 'Who's a lovely girl? Who's a lovely, lovely girl then?'

'How long have you been having problems?' Eimear whispers.

'Eh?'

'You know what I'm talking about. In the bedroom department?'

Arnie wrenches her eyes from the little one to give Eimear a piercing look. 'Is it *that* obvious?'

'You told me he was a virgin when you found him. A forty-year-old virgin. *Yes*, it's that obvious.'

'Yeah, *yeah*. I don't want it spread around, though.'

'No, of course not. I was thinking — how come you haven't started a family yet?'

'Well, like I told you, he never popped the question.'

'I don't think that's required though, is it? These days, couples have children without the aggravation of matrimony.'

'My parents wouldn't allow it... would they? Especially not my daddy.'

'Why not? What's it got to do with him?'

'Oh, didn't you know? My daddy is a big thing in the church. A high-up. I don't know if you know anything about churchy things, but my daddy's an archdeacon... That's one down from the absolute top.'

'I thought Saint Peter was one down from the absolute top!'

Arnie smiles, 'A-Ha! You *do* know about churchy things then? I expect you're catholic.'

'I don't recall you mentioning your father before. I'm not familiar with ranks in the Anglican clergy.'

'He's like a high priest of the diocese. That means he's based in a cathedral.'

'Oh right. Doesn't he have a modern perspective, though? I thought that was why people liked the Anglican church? Because it has a modern outlook — doesn't it?'

Arnie returns the baby to Eimear and allows her arms to hang loose. Eimear notices that her shoulders sag. 'I don't even know if he likes children...' says Arnie.

'Your father?'

'No, *silly*. I'm talking about Nigel. I don't think he likes children. He doesn't share my feelings about a *whole range* of things...'

'What does your dad, the high-priest, think of Nigel?'

'Daddy doesn't like him at all...'

'Why not?'

'He thinks I ought to have landed a younger guy. He thinks I should have landed a bookish type. Daddy had a string of potential suitors lined up...'

'What happened to those suitors?'

'A bunch of lawyers, teachers, academics. I snubbed them.'

'You could adopt, I suppose.'

'What?'

'If you can't have children naturally, I mean — you and Nigel could adopt, couldn't you? Your father couldn't oppose that... could he?

'She's so sweet,' says Arnie. She glances at the baby.

'You love children. It is such a pity you can't have them. I feel sad for you.'

'She reminds me of Rosamund...'

'Rosamund? Who is Rosamund?'

'Oh nobody, nothing. Just a special dolly, that's all. I acquired Rosamund when I was young. I took my dolly, and I played with her in the playhouse. The playhouse that's in the grounds of Colling-wood. That's my father's grace and favour home, by the way. She was lovely.'

'What happened to Rosamund?'

'Gone.'

'Gone?'

'Taken from me.'

'Oh my! How old were you?'

'Nine or ten... I don't remember,' Arnie bites her top lip.

'Did your father take her?'

'Yeah.'

'Why did he do that? Was your father unkind to you?'

'Uh-huh.'

Eimear waited a moment, drew a breath, then she spoke again: 'Why don't you and Nigel adopt?'

Arnie places her palm above her breastbone. 'I guess we can — I never thought about it. '

'Something to discuss, maybe?'

'What?'

'With Nigel?'

'Oh yeah, sure. Anyhow, better get back to the men.'

Arnie provides Eimear with a puny smile as she leaves the room.

'Did you hear all that?' Eimear asks the baby monitor. 'Did you hear it, my love?'

The baby bubbles.

9

Eimear finds Mudgekicker spurting vile bluster on a talk-radio show the following morning. 'There's a vile swarm of unwashed, indestructible aliens coming this way...' says the Mudgekicker. 'A non-indigenous epidemic that seeks to invade our green and pleasant land. In their millions, they come over here.'

'They carry disease with them and bring barbaric laws and laughable culture. They bring their muftis and clerics with them, who will tell you — us — how to eat, pray, and think. We will be told how to act. We will be told how to dress. For example, if you're an English woman, a hijab will be compulsory.'

'We must control and reject this invasive species before it reaches our borders. If we don't halt the tide now, it will be too late.'

'Once they get in — a handful of them to begin with — their rapid reproduction and cunning, underground, habits will mean we're infected in no-time. Certainly, their Eastern ways will have a detrimental impact on our precious traditions.'

'Recent influxes from the East have already stretched our facilities and amenities to breaking point: they mired our hospital services, filled our classrooms, congested our roads, loaded our trains, and overextended our benefits systems. 'Soon, food shortages will be widespread. Meanwhile, all our best jobs are going to this wave of drifters...'

'Like any secretive, grubbing-insects, these invaders seek to penetrate our defences by burrowing under doors. They seek easy openings, you see. They go for unguarded ports. They search for vulnerable gaps. When they find how easy it is to sneak in, they will then antenna their discovery back to the main-body, so, in weeks, a brutish mass will overrun our defences.'

'This is why we have to be careful about every single arrival. No matter how innocent that arrival might seem. The first manifestation of a swarm must be dealt with brutally. We must be vigilant. Or become overwhelmed.'

'When I discovered that a feather-brained elderly chap had unwittingly allowed one of these fledglings into his English home, I knew I had to act. And act swiftly.'

'The soppy old cretin didn't realize that, by giving this hatchling safe harbour, he risked being used. He didn't realize that sending a baby first was a cunning device, designed to violate borders. His misguided 'Christianity' had been exploited.'

'The silly old soul didn't realize that once a creature becomes embedded into society, a full drift of adults will emerge soon after, to claim close relationship with the infant. From that little stream, a mighty flood of unwashed undesirables will flourish.'

'That's how they intend to invade us! Not by force, but by loopholes. We must prevent them! We have to forestall this filthy tide of scum with every muscle, every bone, and every globule of blood we still possess.'

Later, Eimear observes a smart blue four-door saloon draw up outside their house. She sees two stylishly dressed men get out of the vehicle. One brings a clipboard. The other holds what seems to be a radio. The tallest man, the one with the board, reviews documentation and seems to accept that he has arrived at the correct address. He allows the other man to be first to negotiate George's red tile path.

There's a knock on the door. 'George,' Eimear hollers. She appreciates the old man has withdrawn to his workshop to labour on various projects. She tries again, this time louder, '*George...*' she calls, 'There are strange men at the door.'

She hears George tootle to the front-door in carpet slippers. After, she hears the door open and some muttered words along with an assortment of unfamiliar sounds. These sounds, she supposes, are the hisses and crackles of a walkie-talkie. Eimear gets the baby, then goes to the hallway herself, with the baby in her arms.

The taller of the two lofty men leers at her when she emerges. 'Good morning,' he states, giving a lurid wink. It's as if he's trying to pick her up at a wine bar. He looks at the baby and smirks: 'Are you, perhaps, Mr. Florn's granddaughter?'

Eimear returns a flat expression. Her eyes narrow. 'No,' she declares. 'Who are you, dare I ask?'

'Police, ma'am...' says the other. He produces a small card from an internal pocket. 'We are here to take away George Florn.'

'George? But what did he do?' She stares at the old man. 'What have you done?'

'Nothing,' George grumbles. Though the old man sighs as if he had kept a hidden a secret that has suddenly been divulged.

'Your grandfather will come with us...' says the first man

'To help with enquiries,' adds the other.

'Why?' Eimear asks. She looks into their eyes. Nobody, not even George, seems able or inclined to answer this obvious question.

'I need to get my yat and coat,' George mutters. He moves away.

'What's happening?' Eimear asks, under her breath.

'Your grandfather will be back later,' says the tallest man. 'You can come to the station, later, as a visitor, but *not now*. We will have a better chance to chat things over, if you come along to the station in a few hours' time. '

'What things?' she asks.

George collects his hat and coat from pegs. He wobbles the slippers off his ancient toes and pulls his outdoor hush-puppies over thin grey socks.

'Can I take your phone number?' asks the man with the papers. He arches his eyebrow her way.

'If you must... it's on the dial...' Eimear points to the vintage phone on the lobby table. She also offers the young Peeler a cold shoulder.

'What about your mobile, love? That's what I'm after, yeah?' The Peeler glances at their antiquated home-phone and dismisses it with a wave of his fingers. 'Your mobile?'

'What about it?' she asks.

'Fine,' declares the Peeler. 'Have it that way. It's no skin off my nose, if you want to play hard to get, love.'

George plucks his keys from a hook by the door and pulls his hat low, to hide strands of white hair that sprout from his ears. 'Yawl be awright with the young un?' he asks. He provides a feeble grin.

'Yes, George,' she says. She pulls the baby to her breast. 'But you must return by five o'clock, do you hear? Or I will be late for work.'

'That's not gonna happen, love,' says the tall Peeler. 'It will be over when it is over, not before. I would not expect your grandfather to be home before ten, or even midnight.' He gives her a wink then pulls a pair of shiny handcuffs from his back pocket. He clicks the cuffs around George's skinny wrists.

'Is that really necessary?' Eimear asks, with a frown. 'Don't you see he's an old man? He doesn't present any danger. He's not likely to do a runner! Won't you offer him some dignity?'

'Sorry love, it's nothing personal' the officer explains. 'Just procedure. Safe working practices and all that *shitola*. We don't want to do it, but we must.'

'So, to check again, you don't think he'll be back by five?'

'Unlikely, my love.' The Peeler grabs George by the arm. They turn to leave the house.

Eimear hears the front door *slam*. She heads to the front room to watch them take the old man down the garden path. They bundle him into the back of their smart four-door saloon. She also sees the curtains of the house opposite twitch and flicker. Her bitch-landlady sees everything.

'My God,' Eimear remarks to the baby. 'What are we going to do now?'

10

Asif Hussain Zoya is the only Arab tongue who sails aboard the petite fishing boat: CH 31134.

The vessel periodically runs from Cap Du Roc, Harcourt, near the town of Coutances, to the Channel Islands. It is owned and operated by Avelaine Picot. Madame Picot is a wealthy local personage known to everyone as the *Lady Marquesse*. Picot is a proud member of the oldest Manchois family in the region. Commercially, Lady Marquesse runs a six-man rib from Cap Du Roc too. But the rib doesn't see much work *out of season*.

Sailors know the Bay of Mont, or *Cap Du Roc* as it is usually described, as a place that enjoys the highest tides in all Europe. The cape has an exceptional tidal range. According to legend, King William planned his conquest of England from this place. The port lies within a tract of land known as the Forest of Scissy.

Scissy was a mythical demesne that existed until an enormous wave crashed into it, to wash it away from the maps forever. That was in AD 709. Even Mount Tombelaine, the highest point in the forest, was washed into foaming waters. So here, Belenos, god of war and guiding light of the dead, created a portal to the underworld. Belenos chose an appropriate spot.

Le Bar Vacon is the only café in town where a *sheesha* can be blown. So Bar Vacon becomes the foremost meeting place for any number of Algerians, Moroccans, and Tunisians who dwell in the Harcourt vicinity.

Each day, males, gather around short Formica tables at Le Bar Vacon, to bare brown teeth and shrug lop-sided shoulders. They meet to blow *sheesha* pipes and share tittle-tattle from home. North Africans speak French, of course. Likewise, they speak very satisfactory Arabic. But most choose, as an alternative, to prattle to each other in a variety of broken half-cockney English phrases. They're keen to practice this tongue because, one-day, they hope to 'cross the brine' and join friends, family, and neighbours in the paradise across the water. It's a lingo they have evolved by watching too much match-day soccer, British comedy, and episodes of Top Gear. Until a turning point in their conversation, two men had been chatting about *why* a steady stream of migrants continued to risk dangerous sea-crossings to get to *Blighty*.

Zoya's friend, Rakhim, itemized the principal reasons: 'Eish! The ling is already spake. Their gogos and chinas are already living there. Their team already has support. They already glug the soapies. And there are a hundreds other reasons.'

'I committed a mutiny,' Zoya abruptly blurts. 'I make a real good thrill of things but now I mess it up.' Zoya finishes his pungent coffee and moves hands over an almond dish. He decides against taking a sweet and, instead, combs oil-black fingers through wavelets of hair. He looks askance at his pal.

'Why you take the brine in the first place? You ain't no fishy-man, bruv?' Rakhim asks.

Zoya pushes an index finger into his nostril. He blasts a snotty green discharge into the street. 'Because it pay,' he admits. 'I'm a real cool-head guy. I make bread on the water. Good bread. But now I screw-up...'

'No man who rides the sand can ride the tide. It is a known fact...'

offers Rakhim. He polishes his filthy fingernails on yellowed trouser seams.

'Not true,' barks Zoya. 'Our forefathers took the rope and rudder long before the unfaithful grabbed a side-rail and chucked into the brine, ain't it?'

Rakhim chuckles at this because he's heard it told a million times before. But knows it is probably a fable.

'I'm not looking for symphony,' Zoya continues. 'But I'm getting anxious...'

'You'll be fine, little by little, so do not buzz your head with worry,' his friend tells him.

The next day, as foreseen, the grand Marquesse summons Asif Hussain Zoya to her Manchois residence on the outskirts of town. The stronghold is secured by basalt palisades, with high crenelated walls, and is adorned with elegant ridges.

After negotiating a wrought iron gateway fitted with ultra-modern electronic access controls, guards urge Zoya into the main body of the house. A liveried servant directs him to an antechamber. Zoya hangs around the waiting place and he regards the tapestries. He secretly judges the room to be poorly equipped because there is nothing of pocketable value.

At the proper time, a dumpy white woman emerges. Zoya regards her well-groomed hazel hair, recently glossed lips, and sparkling sapphire earrings. Zoya spies a gilded wristwatch upon her cuff and watches as it jangles. He imagines he might easily snatch the treasure away from this lady in a blink. He licks his lips.

'You speak English, yes?' the lady says, her cobalt eyes glowing with confidence. Her bold manner places him off guard.

Zoya wrests his eyes from her elegant timepiece. He takes a breath, then fixes her eyes. 'Where is Bo Runner?' he asks.

'That is what I want to know *from you*. It's why I asked you here.

Have you seen him? He works for *me*. He is missing. You will explain where he has gone...'

'I last saw the master of the baghlah on our recent sea-voyage. Why ask me, mistress? I cannot speak for the Captain! And I don't know where he might be, 'specially when ashore. I really don't know where he is...'

'Sit down. Tea?'

'May I stand?'

'No, you may *not*.'

Avelaine Picot rings a porcelain bell and tea is brought. She points to a seat, then perches her pleats into an upholstered chair opposite. She urges Zoya to settle, but finds he is ill at ease in her company. He is altogether self-conscious. His shabby chemise smells to high-heaven, his thin Carrefour-branded jeans are sullied by fish-oil, and his threadbare body-warmer is greased by sea-vapour and secretions.

Once the tea-tray arrives, Avelaine Picot invites Zoya to speak. He knows he must choose his next words *very* attentively. 'I try hard not to bemoan what you want me to say ' he explains. His hand wobbles as he takes the saucer from her manicured fingers. He tries not to spill the beverage or tip sideways her expensive bone china. 'But you see, I have not seen Bo Runner since our last expedition. I do not know why you ask me. Please, lady, I cannot account for another sailor's comings and goings.'

'You already said *all those* things.' Lady Marquesse shakes her head to demonstrate that repetition displeases her. 'Tell me something *else*. Tell me something *new*. For example, when, upon that voyage, did you last see his living face?'

'Mistress? I don't know what you mean by such a question. All I can tell you is that Bo Runner returned to shore with me. That was the last I saw of him...'

'Are saying he returned from the Cap Du Roc?'

'Of corpse he did. He wished me to steer the craft in, and that's what I did. I did what was asked. At sea we hoisted the jaunty flag as one, and we brung it down too, once the mission was over here at port. This is exactly as your instructions. We motored into dock. The last time I saw Bo Runner was when he roped your craft at this quayside.'

'Are you sure?' asks Avelaine Picot. She fixes her eyes on the man's temples.

'Yes sure-as-sure can be. How else can a sea-craft come in? One mariner must steer, another must rope. It is a two-man enterprise. It's the way of things. Two men are required to bring a boat to port.'

The lady throws Zoya a stony expression. Then abruptly changes her line of questioning: 'Do you know why we throw them adrift at Point Blanc?'

'Hew?'

'Don't say *hew*, it's not a proper word...' She reprimands him with a scowl. 'Do you know why we cast the travellers adrift at that specific point? I am asking because I want to find out how much you know and how much you understand...'

'Is it because the coastguard and hearing station is at Saint Helier?'

'Yes, it is *exactly* that reason. You are not an idiot, are you?' The lady allows him a thin smile. 'It's a procedure we worked out long ago. And it worked for months. You will not mess things up now, will you?'

'No, my Lady Marquesse. What has this to do with the disappearance of Bo Runner?'

'I wonder whether he doubted it. I wonder if he doubted our procedure. Did he, for example, reveal misgivings to you? Perhaps he thought it's not civilised to deposit travellers into the brine at Point Blanc. Perhaps because he thought it was too far from their destination...'

'No mistress. He did not give me such doubts. Are you thinking that Bo Runner split because he has been ouch-ooing his head about such things?'

'Try to use proper English words and expressions, or don't bother at all.' Lady Marquesse gives Zoya an irascible gaze. 'I had my doubts about the Captain's state-of-mind. When we first decided to cast them adrift at Point Blanc, he argued, saying it was *not humane*. What do you think? I want your honest opinion about Bo Runner's state of mind. La Corbière does not suspect anything, or they would have informed me. Our system is safe. For now, anyway. But tell me this, Zoya, did the Captain squeeze his luck? Or did you?' The lady places her saucer onto the side-table and makes a tut-ting noise. She glares deep into Zoya's eyes: 'I think *something* happened out there in the waters. Did one of you got cold-feet? Perhaps you? Did you aggravate him?'

'No mistress, I never did squeeze my luck. Do you mean with Bo Runner? No, I never did...I never did abnegate nobody.' Zoya's saucer vibrates in his fingers. 'Why would I? He is a good skipper...'

'Maybe you fell out. Or bickered over payments. Such things can happen at sea. You can tell me, I would understand... Perhaps Bo Runner fell into the water... or maybe he was drunk on liquor and toppled into the brine, blind drunk. Is that what happened? Or you did you have a rumpus, and he got knocked in by mistake? Perhaps that is how it happened. You might as well come clean... I will not punish you if you tell me the truth... but I *will* punish you if you lie.'

'No mistress, he didn't fall into the brine. Bo Runner is a most experian sailor. He knows all about boats and can do it in his sleep. He is a very experian man...'

'Then his disappearance is a mystery...' the Lady Marquesse folded her arms. 'I do not like mysteries. So, to put my mind at rest, tell me how the voyage unfolded. Did you get to Point Blanc?'

The incompatible odd-couple sit in awkward silence, before Zoya ventures: '*Yes*, mistress, we got to Point Blanc.'

'And did you drop the cargo at the place we agreed?'

'Yes.'

'The exact place? Please confirm that you cast eight souls adrift at the *agreed* place?'

'Yes. There was a baby in the group. And a mother...'

Avelaine Picot raises a hand to protest. 'It makes no difference who they were. I just want to be sure we delivered them *beyond* Point Blanc. You say that we did, yes?'

'Yes, of corpse.'

'And was Bo Runner present when the cargo was deposited at the agreed place?'

'Yes.'

'So you were both present when the cargo was dropped into the ocean, yes? And you both watched them float away, beyond Point Blanc?' The lady examines his face, with unblinking eyes.

'Yes, Lady Marquesse — beyond the Point.'

'And afterwards, you both returned to Cap Du Roc?'

'Yes, mistress, as I already said.'

'Both you and Bo Runner brought the craft into port, and both roped her?'

'Yes, mistress.'

'Is that the last time you saw the captain?'

'Yes.' Zoya rubs hollow cheeks with grubby fingers.

'So that's it then...you've been a blameless worker. That's why I've decided to give you a chance to better yourself. You will take my craft on her next voyage — you will act as her captain. How do you like that? You'll need to find another seafarer, mind. Someone who can help you with rope and tie. You should recruit a suitable deckhand. You'll need to do that *right away*. It must be someone who can keep his mouth shut. Do you understand?'

'Oh yes, mistress.'

'Oh, and there's one more thing...' The Lady rises. She takes her tinkle-bell. Zoya recognizes his presence is no longer required. 'I asked Paw-Claw to investigate the disappearance of Bo Runner. I asked him to get to the bottom of the mystery,' she declares.

'Paw-Claw?' Zoya cries. He gives her a terrified glance.

'You know of him?'

'Everyone knows Paw-Claw, mistress. Is it really necessary to bring him? He's a dread...'

'Yes, I think it is necessary because we must get this affair solved.

Don't you think? There's a lot at stake, don't you agree? If the former Skipper divulges our activities, we have much to lose, don't we? So I require Paw-Claw to complete a thorough investigation. For your sake, for my sake, for all our sakes. Do I make myself clear?'

'Oh yes, mistress.'

'So I invited Paw-Claw to probe. He will get to the bottom of things. He will not be satisfied until he finds the missing Bo Runner and *extinguishes* him. Do you understand? We need to be sure we have secured Bo Runner's silence...'

Zoya nods. He directs his gaze to the floorboards, in soundless acquiescence. Though, at that moment, he thinks about something else entirely.

Zoya thinks about the lady's six-man rib.

Zoya nibbles his remaining fingernails and smokes a Gitanes through an open window. He watches gulls dip in an easterly breeze. Leaf-shaped clouds build on the horizon, so he knows he has only thirty-six hours to complete an escape. Zoya plans to take the rib to the Cape, and thereafter, beyond, to a land of sanctuary. Once beyond the Cape, fate will decide what happens.

The Lady Marquesse asked him to look for a deckhand. He discards such an idea with a finger-tap to his nose: he will *not* need help with *the rib*, will he? He'll use a powerful motor, dead of night, once he's oared the rib from port, soundlessly, to take the tide. It won't be easy, but he knows it is possible. He's sure his plan will work. He knows he'll have to navigate past Point Blanc, on the far side of La Corbière. That was the genius part of his plan: the rib ran low and was too small for detection. And the assembly materials of a rib are transparent to coastal radar.

Zoya contemplates his chewed fingertips and admits he feels nervous. He's anxious because of the imminent arrival of Paw-Claw.

Paw-Claw's outrageous misdeeds are fabled across the East. They say he sliced off a lady's breasts when he discovered, on behalf of her intended husband, she was *not* a virgin. Another time, he hanged a thief from a gallows-tree after Paw-Claw had proven the man stole funds from an employer. And they said Paw-Claw had slain two sisters who slept together. He had placed their bodies into identical mailbags, loaded the bags with shingle, then dumped the bags into a well. He also disabled an inadequate suitor, a bachelor, who'd been seducing a low-birth unbeliever. On that occasion, he'd hacked the man's big-toes from his feet, using gardening shears. He'd even attacked a professional soldier! On that occasion he'd confronted the perpetrator with a pickaxe, after he discovered the soldier had lied to betters. The soldier's friends later found his body on the roadside, quartered. All these stories, and more, were *true*. Zoya lit another cigarette and rubbed his dirty palms over filthy temples. Thirty-six hours remaining. Would Paw-Claw arrive before he had a chance to sail?

At the cafe, Zoya confides in his pal, Rakhim: 'I went to see Lady Marquesse. She summoned me...'

Rakhim nods. He moves his hand to his neck, to scratch the wind-pipe. 'Was it to speak about the mutiny you committed?' asks Rakhim. He poses the question with the candid expression of a child.

Zoya turns silent for a moment. He considers his pal's gormless features and wonders whether he told his chum *too much* the last time they met. But after the voyage, he'd felt a terrible burden, the pressure of it had made him giddy with worry... so he decided to get things off his chest. Because the worry weighed-him-down like a sea-anchor. Telling his friend felt like an unshackling. It needed to be done. But now Zoya saw things more soberly and guessed he might have divulged *too much*. So he decided to twist things around: 'It's a doggy-dog world...' he points out. He gives a wrinkled sigh. Zoya crosses lanky limbs under the table. 'Maybe I should not have told you about such things. I do not want to put your life into danger.'

'Danger?' shouts Rakhim. His eyes bulge. His mouth opens. 'Why would I be in danger?'

Zoya waves a trembling hand across his pal's face. Then he stiffens his collar-muscles, before he adopts a shorter voice, 'We must use careful words, my friend. We must keep our voices low. Above all, we must remain alert...'

'Alert? Why?' Rakhim produces a suppressed cry. He frowns and shoots Zoya a piercing look.

'They are sending Paw-Claw. Ordering him to investigate.'

Rakhim runs a finger across his grimy forehead, to wipe away a line of sweat. 'Are you kidding with my leg?' He grabs the side of the table. His knuckles go white.

'Have you heard of Paw-Claw?' asks Zoya, seeing his pal's reaction.

'Everyone's heard of Paw-Claw,' Rakhim says. 'You are in deep shit and worse. You are going to get smashed...'

'*Shhh*. Look at me, *look at me*...' Zoya pulls his friend close, a brawny hand around a scrawny neck. 'There is no need to get nervous. I can keep *you* out of this. When Paw-Claw asks how you are involved, I will say I don't know nothing...'

'Keep me out of it?' Rakhim widens his eyes. 'Keep me out of what? I am not involved in nothing. I haven't got involved in your shit. I didn't do anything. Why would Paw-Claw ask about me? I am in total innocence.'

'Well, no, you're not innocent, *actually*, ' Zoya drops a shoulder and gives a dejected sigh. 'Metrically speaking, this is very cantillated, but Paw-Claw will consider you an accessory. Don't you see that? Yes, you are implicated, up to your neck.'

'Me? I didn't accessorize nothing. I didn't accessorize no shit...'

'But I told you, didn't I? I spoke about the...' Zoya moves close to whisper: 'I told you about the *mutiny*... it makes you an accessory after the fact...'

'But, *but*...' Rakhim wipes froth from his forehead. 'But I did not tell no body. Really, I never did! Not a livid soul.'

'Exactly...'shouts Zoya with a triumphant smile. He gives his pal a gesture of approval. 'And for such loyalty, Paw-Claw will judge you. He will accuse you of *aiding*. Precisely because you did not tell anyone. You had the opportunity to explain about the mutiny to authorities, but you decided to stay *scutum*. Paw-Claw will not like that at all, will he? He will take your silence as approval...'

'Approval? But I don't approve no shit. What can we do?'

'We must stay firm. We must keep our heads down. When Paw-Claw arrives, we must be ready for bitter interrogation.'

'My zarumba! Interrogation? Have you ever seen him before? What is he like?'

'No, I never seen him before,' Zoya shakes his head. 'I imagine he is a great brute of a man, with frayed black thawb, a lengthy goat-hair agal upon a tall head. No doubt, he'll arrive armed with a gigantic golden nimcha, worn at the waist.'

Rakhim closes his eyes and issues a small moan. 'What will we do when he comes?'

'We'll burn that bridge when we come to it...'

'Can't you curry flavour with Lady Marquesse? Can't you get her to call Paw-Claw off?'

'It is too late for that. She told me he's coming...'

'My zarumba,' Rakhim says. He scans the tables to examine other diners. 'He could be any one of these eaters. What if Paw-Claw is *already* here? You might be sliced into pieces by sunset. What do we *actually* know about Paw-Claw?'

'Not much. I ain't never seen a picture of him. I don't think nobody ever has. I just heard folk tales... the same ones you have heard. No, I don't think he's here yet because the lady Marquesse didn't say so...' Zoya pauses for thought, then he continues. 'He's a successful man, certainly. I guess he wouldn't dine here, not in a shit hole. I guess he's aged about thirty. But not younger. Most of those guys are in their thirties.' Zoya looks around the café.

'And he's a Mohammedan?'

'Needless to say. So it rules out greasy *minchos*. And he must be physically large because he heaves sacks into wishing wells...'

Rakhim gives an involuntary shake. Then he asks: 'Is he rich?'

'I suppose he must be. He will travel by car, no doubt, not in the back of a truck. I expect he'll use a Mercedes Bends, that's what all the rich use. He'll have plenty of bucks to splash, so I guess he will stay at our top-most hotel...'

'The Beausejour?' suggests Rakhim.

'Definitely. The best place in town. He'll eat the finest food. And will go to see the Lady Marquesse...'

'Yes, I suppose he will,' concedes Rakhim.

'I hadn't thought of these things before. He will need to get a briefing from the mansion. We should keep a casual eye on the hotel and the Marquesse residence. To see if a Mercedes Bends visits...'

'Yes,' says Rakhim. He delivers a firm nod. He feels ready to lift his cup to dry lips. 'Then we will *do him...*'

'What?' Zoya cries. He throws his pal a sickened glance. 'What do you mean, *do* him?' Zoya shuffles his toes under the table.

'It's obvious,' explains Rakhim. 'We are between rock and a heartache — there is only one way to end this shit — otherwise Paw-Claw will persecute us forever. We have to *do him* before he does us.'

'Are you suggesting we put an end to him?'

'Yes,' says Rakhim, his mind now set. 'He's digging his own nest by coming here. It will be his *comeuppins*. We must make vengeance before he vengeances us...'

'Well, I'm not sure,' Zoya rubs his neck. 'He is a remarkable executioner and skilled inquisitor. I don't think we will get the upper hand. He will get the better of us...

'Oh, we can handle Paw-Claw. We will *do him* when the time is ripe. You have the brains. I have the balls. You can watch the hotel. I will watch the mansion. We'll grab him before he goes to see the Lady. When we see him, we'll *do him*. What time do you think he will arrive?'

'After noon, I suppose. He will travel in the cool light of morning and arrive after lunch, before afternoon prayer. That's how the wealthy always arrive.'

'In that case, we will start our vigil tomorrow, after the noon-day sun..."

11

At one o'clock, on the following afternoon, Zoya finds himself loitering outside Hotel Beauséjour. It's regarded as the best lodging in Harcourt. He's anticipating the arrival of Paw-Claw.

It bothers that him he talked himself into such a mess. He pinches his arm with sticky fingers. There was already much to do and little time to achieve it, without getting involved in this *absurd* farce. He felt this idiotic plan nibbled into the precious time he had left before the next tide. Zoya wished to check the motor on the 6-man rib. He wanted to be sure it was greased and wanted to confirm that the craft was serviceable. He needed to feed the fuel tank and steal extra marine gasoline. He required oars too, and supposed they'd had to be stolen from the dock. He also lacked charts. Where could he steal those? This was a onetime opportunity to break-out, and he didn't want to miss anything *crucial*.

But his idiot pal delayed all those sensible preparations by producing a crazy-stupid plan to 'do' Paw-Claw. 'It's not rocket surgery,' Rakhim suggested when they met at noon and before they took their stake-out respective positions. 'Once he arrives, we will take Paw-Claw to the dockside. There, we will explain we have something to present. He will be curious. You will provide false statements and confusing information to throw him off his senses... then I will clabber him with a meat hammer...' At that point Rakhim produced a food tenderizer from his waist-band. 'This is what I employ to clabber beef-steaks in the kitchen. I will clabber him with this hammer, and we will throw his body in the water. When authorities find him, they will think he tripped on a mooring post, knocked his head on a quayside lip, and he drowned in the terrible inky depths...'

Once Zoya nodded, Rakhim suggested they send a text as soon as either one glimpsed Paw Claw. "When will it be done?' Zoya had asked. He had glanced at the old-clock on the town hall.

'It will be over when it finish,' Rakhim had told him.

At five past three, a man, likely of Liberian descent, sticks his long legs from the back-seats of a super-shiny Citroën that pulls up outside the posh hotel. The man stretches his legs. No doubt he's tired after the long journey. He collects luggage from the tail-gate, two Louis Vuitton branded push-along cases. After that, he produces a large roll of banknotes from a trouser pocket and pays off the driver. He jingles a platinum-tinted wristwatch as Zoya watches him peel away a large denomination euro-note from his bankroll, to give to the taxi-man as a tip. The driver shows he's pleased by smiling. Then the Liberian gentleman adjusts a pair of gold-framed spectacles upon his nose before he wanders into the hotel lobby, pulling his shabby-chic suitcases behind. Zoya guesses the man is thirty, grey hair, oval face. He has dark skin and a powerful body.

Zoya is about to text Rakhim to inform him. Then he decides a message isn't suitable for what he needs to say. So he calls him: 'I just saw Paw-Claw. He arrived a minute ago.' His pa has an excited tone. 'The geezer came to town in a big car and had a lot of cash. He meets our requirements. I reckon it's him.'

'Good,' says Rakhim. 'Are you sure this is the guy?'

'Well, he is a stranger in town, and he fits the pro-vile so, yes, pretty much....'

Rakhim sings: 'Today is gonna be the day that we're gonna put a tag on you...' The tune is *Wonderwall*, by Oasis.

'What do you want me to do?' Zoya asks, interrupting the song.

'Is he gone inside yet?'

'Yup.'

'Don't let him get to the Lady Marquesse. Don't let him get to her mansion. If he heads her way, we must do everything we can to vivisect him.'

'What if he calls a taxi?'

'Then you must stop the car. Make-out you're sick or something. Think on your fleet...'

'Okay. But what are you going to do?'

'I will meet you at the hotel. We will wait together and see what he does. Then we will former-mate a plan. Know what I mean?'

'I'm going to have to hang here?'

'Yes, stay outta sight, in cakes he looks out the window to check it is all-clear. He's a slippery sneakadoo. We cannot be too careful...'

'That is true. I will sneak back into a dark alley. I will keep watch on the main door.'

'I'll be over in a thrice."

Thirty-five minutes later Rakhim looms into the alleyway. His yellow teeth shine. There is a smile on his lips.

'You seem cheerful,' Zoya remarks. His pal is peculiarly happy.

'I love it when a plan comes together,' Rakhim says. 'Any movement from Paw-Claw yet?' He turns his gaze to the hotel windows across the square. 'I suppose he has one of the best rooms on the top floor. They have the biggest and cleanest rooms in the pen-house.'

'I suppose,' Zoya replies. But he feels disconcerted by his pal's perkiness. So creases his brows as he tries to focus his gaze on the upper windows of the hotel. 'How long do you think we have to do this?' he asks.

'I don't know. He might pop out before afternoon prayer. We

should be ready to dash the road. To stop him, if he come out...' With those words, Rakhim begins a series of exercises. He positions close to the green fern wall and bends a leg, keeping a foot flat on the cobblestone. He holds a gymnastic pose for sixty seconds before he takes a big step forward with his left foot, to bend a knee. He keeps the right leg straight, then, with both sets of blotty fingers, he points straight ahead. For another sixty seconds, he does this pose. Then Rakhim revolves his shoulder-blades and loosens his arms. 'What you staring at?' he asks Zoya. 'You supposed to be watching the hotel...'

'I'm sorry,' Zoya murmurs. He turns his gaze from his pal to view the building. He rubs his nose.

Once he has completed his exercises, Rakhim joins Zoya at the entrance to the alley. They push remarkably close to make the most of shadows. Zoya feels the heat and dampness from his pal's skin. 'Really, you and I are one in the same, aren't we? Rakhim suggests, in breathy tones.

'You think?' Zoya replies. 'How do you figure ?'

'Two streetwise comrades, brothers, both with bad reputations and unstable moral compasses. The continent of our character rather than the colour of our skin, will be our judgement... yes, we are a couple of dodgy fellows.'

Zoya wrinkles his nose at this observation: 'I was not always like this, you know. I wasn't always discreditable. I wasn't always hanging around drab alleys, plotting murder. Once I was an upright, honest and re-spectacle worker. I was a big-man in the structural architect's office of ancient Sanaa. I had a salary, a pension, a girlfriend, a career prospect and even my own apart-en-ment.'

'Really? Did you work in oil?'

'Ealing-Gee. Natural gas liquefaction...'

'You had a big cushy life? A big-man industrial?' Rakhim snorts. He wiggles his brows. He gives Zoya a hearty, and brotherly, slap on the back. 'You were a corporate guy, and I didn't even know... man, what happened to you, bruv?'

'Yeah...' Zoya glances at his oil-stained jeans and cheap trainers.

He hunches his shoulders: 'I am pathetic, aren't I? I toiled in a giant draughtsman's office and I worked on the designs the sketchers gave, making three-dimensional samples so bosses see'd what to do next...'

'Neat, how did you get into that line of work? You go to collage?'

'I already mastered skills as a woodcarver and learned to read at Ealing-Gee. The company trained me to capture designs. I fashioned wood samples from drawings.'

'So you were a wood modeller in Sanaa?'

'Something like that...' Zoya gives a sigh. 'My occupation was patternmaker. But one thing led to another, it was like a landslide of dominoes... the drawing shop closed. Ealing-Gee sold the business to Chinese. We had big problems with Arabia. You know the rest because of world-news. I left everything I worked hard to achieve and escaped so I wouldn't suffer harm.'

'You leave family?'

Zoya nodded silently yet said nothing.

'So you ended in this...'

'Yes, exactly.'

'What do you wanna do next, brother? Go back to Sanaa?'

'I never want to go there again...' Zoya shudders at the memory. 'I want to cross the water, find peace. Later, when I settle, I will retrieve my family and bring them to Blighty.'

'Is that why you become a fishy-man? So you would learn to steer a boat across the brine?'

'I went to the port one day and Bo Runner came to me, and he said, 'Do you want to work?' I said, 'Of course. But, sorry boss, I ain't never done deck work before.' Bo Runner said: 'It is great, son. It's easy as falling off a dog —why you not try it?' I said, 'No way, boss, I have not got the sea-eggs.' Bo Runner says, 'You do not need see-eggs where we go! In this boat all we do is trip around the bay, nothing more. I do not really sail; I do pleasure boating.' So he offered me a job. I accept because I have nothing better to do.'

'And you work for Bo Runner ever since?'

'That was ten months ago. Things were good to start. We caught fish with nets. We wobbled in steady-water around the bay. Bo

Runner teached me to rope and take wheel. When I was good enough to be dependable, he let the other guy go. He pay him off, never to sea again. Then Bo Runner told me we'd go on a *foray*. I didn't know what *foray* meant. The next day, on the tide, we sailed beyond Jersey Bailliage.'

'What happened?'

'Nothing! We turned back. It was a big waste of time. I thought it was a pointless voyage. Later, I figured Bo Runner had been testing things... checking the British sensors and detection systems. We did not do the actual *foray* until three days after that, at nightfall. On the *real* voyage we took six African men, under tired-paulines. When we reached the point where we turned around before, then we threw them in the water.'

'Threw them? Threw the men? You drowned them?'

'No, we cast them. Lowered them into the inflate-tables. Three souls in each. We bought the inflate-tables at the beach-shop. Yes, I know what you are thinking. I doubt they survived. Maybe they did, maybe they didn't. Who knows? But I can say with true-heart that it is lonely weather out there, waves are large beyond the Point, and sea is icy. Yet those men were *happy* to go into the brine, even though their inflate-tables wobbled. They were *happy* to go! We were well rewarded too, me and Bo, when we got back. We got good pay for the drop. We took the craft to port and the next night we collected a different six men and did it all over again...'

'And this happened every night?'

'Just three nights in a row. When tide is right. Then nothing.'

'Why nothing?'

'When the tide is dry on the Bay of Mont, the current is gone. You can only take a boat-out three nights in a row. You are high-and-dry for thirty-six hours...'

'You are high-and-dry now? This is one of those times?'

'Yes. But I have much to do. Preparations and so forth...'

'Don't you get paid when you are high-and-dry?'

'Nope.'

'Is that why you did a mutiny?'

'I would rather not talk about it...'

'But things get difficult, okay?' Rakhim wipes his runny nose on a sleeve and offers a broad smile, 'Every man has a story. It does not matter how difficult things get; it adds character.'

Zoya sniffs, 'I suppose.'

At five-twenty, a tall black man emerges from the hotel lobby. They see that the guy is dressed in light-cotton, emerald-coloured pants with a blue grandfather shirt. He wears a white prayer-hat on his dark head. He sports a tummy that resembles a spare tyre. Zoya decides it's his snack-belly. 'I think that is him...' says Zoya. He thumbs an ear and shuffles.

Both men move from their concealed position. They do not take their eyes off the black man. 'Are you sure?' Rakhim mutters. 'He looks a bit silly. A bit flabbish. He does not look like a mackerel born killer.'

'He changed. He changed into light clothes...'

'And grew a belly?'

'I didn't see it before. But I recognise his glasses and wristwatch. It is a good watch. This is the same man who came by Citroën.'

They hurry to the side of the hotel. But it does not look like Paw-Claw wants to take the taxi. In fact, he glances down the street and starts striding toward the church.

'Where is he going?' asked Rakhim. 'It isn't the way to the Mansion.'

'He wants a bite to eat...'

'We will follow.'

Zoya and Rakhim allow Paw-Claw to leave first, and then trail him. It is clear the man has never been to Harcourt before, and so seems unsure which way to walk. On one occasion, he doubles-back. Rakhim stoops behind a bush, while Zoya hides in a doorway. After, they follow the contract-man to the town's modest market, where he slows to look into windows. 'He reads menus...' Rakhim remarks.

Paw-Claw settles on an eatery and goes to an empty table. He lowers his bulk into a metal-framed bistro chair at a place called La Table de Michel. Scallops are a specialty of the house, along with fresh prawns and *moules*. 'Why did he choose that place? They vend seafood...'

'He'll order duck. They do good duck.'

'Did you ever ate it?'

'No, I never did. It is *tres* expensive at Michel's'

'That's fine then, this must be our man, huh?' Rakhim rubs his finger and thumb to demonstrate their marked man is wealthy. 'He has a lot of mullahs, yes? We will watch what he does from a table by the Tabac.'

'Good idea. They sell tea?'

'We can sit and discover if they do.'

They pull slimy chairs from an ivy-covered wall and position themselves by a wrought table at the Tabac. They move their bodies to face Paw-Claw, who is sitting opposite. They watch as Paw-Claw orders bread and water. He speaks good French. Several minutes pass before an elderly woman approaches their table. She gives them a cloudy look and says, with an accompanying growl: 'Ce que tu veux boire?'

'Thé?' Zoya asks.

'Pas probable. Nous avons eu de la bière, nous avons eu du soda, nous avons eu un bol de cidre ou de vin rouge. Ou de l'eau. Vous voulez de l'eau minérale?'

'Water,' Zoya decides. Rakhim nods.

'Paw-Claw is drinking le vin,' remarks Zoya. He is horrified by the man's behaviour. They see Paw-Claw's uniformed server bring a green bottle wrapped in a white towel. The waiter pours golden liquor into a long-stemmed, bowl-shaped glass. Paw-Claw takes a sip.

'Really?' says Rakhim. 'Do you sit in a seafood store and gobble fermented beverages Mister Fat Man?'

'Seems he does.'

'So much for being a Muhammadan,' remarks Rakhim.

'Maybe he is not strict. Like me. Sometimes I drink a cold beer... sometimes a beer calms my throat like nothing else.'

'Whatever floats your goat,' says Rakhim. 'You never seize to amaze me...'

Zoya takes these words as a compliment. He pulls a pack of smokes from his thigh pocket. 'You never told me what you do...' he declares. He lights up. 'I told you everything about me, where I came from, what I did, but you kept shtum. I have been your pal you for a month, but I don't know nothing about who you are. I don't even know your faction...'

'Me? I come from East...'

'They all say that...'

'Ha! They do, true. But none come from East like I do, bruv. I am from Sogdiana...'

'I never heard of it...'

'You heard of Samarqand, yes?'

'The Registan?'

'You are a smart guy...'

'I studied architecture.'

'Yes, you did. And it is good we are conversating about it now, yes?'

The water is delivered, though they notice the miserable old lady slams the bottle on the table.

'What are you doing in Harcourt?'

'Me?' asks Rakhim, 'I work in the kitchen. I thought I showed you my meat hammer.'

'But...' Zoya wrinkles his brow and bites his top lip. 'How come you are never working? I met many kitchen-men, and they all worked hours-upon-hours.'

'This is my free day.'

'And yesterday?'

'Okay, *okay*, you grabbed me. I got fired. To be honest, my answers were prayed because I hated the place where I worked up till now. I am between jobs.'

'Which place was it?'

'The kitchen where I worked? The *Balade* in Galette, near Gambetta, you know it?'

'No I never did...'

'Do not go there, it is a shit hole. Believe me.'

'So why did you come all the way *here* from Samarqand?'

'What, me? Looking for adventure, I suppose.'

'And did you find it?'

'Oh yes.'

'Since they laid you off, what are you going to do?'

'I don't know...' Rakhim watches Paw-Claw tie a plastic bib around his neck. 'My zarumba,' he blurts. 'The pig is about to eat shells!'

'The reason I ask,' continues Zoya. 'Is that they have asked me to hire a deckhand for my next trip.'

'Not me bruv. I cannot swim. Plus, also, I am agoraphobic to water...'

'I think that really means open spaces. The word agoraphobic means fear of open spaces.'

'Exactly, bruv, and there is no space more open than the ocean, is there? Am I right?'

'I suppose you are. Well, maybe you could help me on dry land...'

'Go on, bruv...'

'I need help. *Tonight.* To get equipment together and prepare my next voyage. Would you help? There is fifty euros in it. Plus, I guarantee no swimming required.'

'I will think about it. But first we have to deal with that guy over there. One of us should go across, once he has done filling his snout, and chat with him...'

'Really?'

'Yes, it should be you. Because you are the one who went to *collage.* Go over when he's fed his gut and make idol conservations. Talk to him about that and this. Then you must say something curious. Say something remarkable that lures him to the dock...'

'Lures him?'

'Yes, bruv, you're the fishy-man so you know what *lures* means doesn't you? We need to get him by the docks so we can clobber the daylights out of him...' Rakhim pulls the end of the meat hammer from his waistband, to reinforce the point.

'Yes, I suppose you are right,' Zoya says. He gives a sad nod.

'He is about to call the server...' says Rakhim, a twinkle in his eye. 'Now is your chance to lure him to the jetty for a bashing...'

Zoya returns a vacant stare and licks his lips. 'Are you sure we should do this?'

'Yes, I'm very sure we discussed it, right? It's him or us...'

So Zoya rises from the table at the Tabac. With quivering limbs, he walks as nonchalantly as he can, towards the Table de Michel. Behind him he hears the old woman leave the door of her shop to talk loudly to Rakhim about payment for their table water, though he fixes his gaze on Paw-Claw. The fat guy does not seem to notice his impending approach. When he's within spitting range of the chubby fellow, Zoya coughs to announce his presence. The man looks up to see who dares bother him at his table.

'Parlez vous anglais?' Zoya says. He gives the guy a generous smile.

'Yes, why?' replies Paw-Claw.

'I have a proposition...'

'Are you English?' says the fat-man. 'You do not seem very English to me...'

'I am a sea traveller, sir. I come from here and I come from there. I travel forth. I come from no place special. '

'Well, if it is all the same with you, — whoever you are and wherever you might be from — I don't wish to be disturbed by a man of your character. So, be off...'

'Please sir, you have not heard my proposition yet...'

'And I care not to. I do not like to be approached by strangers. I especially don't like to be approached by strangers when I'm eating. So please take your bid and leave me in peace...'

'I see you are a man of superior appetite wanting the best in flavour... but I also noticed you had finished dining.'

Paw-Claw nods. He sucks in his cheeks, and squints. Zoya senses the man is becoming unsettled, so concludes he must produce something *quick,* or the moment will pass: 'I'll get straight to the point.'

'I wish you would...' says Paw-Caw. He takes his eyes from Zoya and removes a large roll of notes from a back pocket. He slaps a flat fifty on the table. Zoya sees an elegant watch glint on the man's arm.

'I guess you're a quality food and five-star wine lover,' Zoya continues. 'I thought I would come over to offer you a luxury product...'

'Why would I want a product from you?' Paw-Claw looks him up and down and produces an expression of disgust. 'To be honest, monsieur, you look like a reprobate and fraudster. I would rather have *nothing* to do with you...'

'Me Sir? No, not me, sir. You are confusing me with another fellow. I'm a simple seafaring man. With a tale to tell and an offer to make...'

'Tell me your tale promptly and then be off, scélérat.'

'But Monsieur, for me to tell my tale I must first show you the goods I found...'

'What did you find?'

'On my travels, I discovered a quantity of Remy Martin. Singular and rare bottles of brandy. Have you heard of the marque?'

'*Everyone* has heard of Remy Martin. It's not extraordinary... You are wasting my time.'

'Each of the bottles I found is preserved inside its own wooden presentation box along with a cut-glass cup. If you come with me, you'll see that each box is marked in English: *XO Fine Champagne Cognac...* is that good, I wonder? Since I do not drink the stuff, I'm not an expert. It is why I need an authority like you to come to inspect the goods. Is this valuable?'

'Yes, XO is an utterly delicious mouthful. You don't drink?'

'No sir. Which is why I want someone to take the bottles off my hands. I would prefer my cognac to go to someone who has a good palate and is well-bred and might appreciate it. Nobody around these parts drinks' libation of such quality. When I saw you, I recognised a true connoisseur. Would you make an offer for all four bottles? I am thinking they are worth four hundred...a hundred each.'

Paw-Claw lifts his nose at such an exorbitant suggestion: 'How big are the bottles?' he asks with a sniff. 'I mean to say, that quote seems high, since they might be fakes...'

'It says seventy centilitres on each bottle. Each box contains a certificate of authenticity. I would be most happy to crack open a bottle for you to take a sip, sir, if you must. If I did, however, you must agree to take *that* bottle. How does such an offer sound? Is it fair? If you taste a sip, I'm sure you will make an offer for the remaining bottles.'

'Well, that's good of you. I suppose it is fair...' Paw-Claw licks his lips at the idea. 'Naturally, I would need to taste the spirit, to validate and verify the truth of your claim, and to be sure it's XO as you say. I would choose one bottle at random, to make a tasting. Yes? But even if I approve of the spirit, I will give only you *two hundred* in cash for four bottles. That is fifty a bottle. Does that sound reasonable?'

Zoya gives a half-hearted shrug and exhales, 'I expected a little more, to be honest, but you are the expert. I wanted to push you beyond two-fifty. But you are a first-class negotiator. I have a big ruck-sack in my lock-store that you could use to take- away the bottles. Shall we fetch the cognac now?'

'What is the hurry Monsieur? I am in town for two more nights. I'm here on business. I can collect those bottles any time. At this late hour, I would prefer not to knock about a dark quayside. I'm easily agitated, do you see? I prefer to conduct my business in daylight...'

'Well, that is the thing, sir — it's true you may be around for two days, but I *will not*. I'm off on my next voyage. Right away, actually. I am taking the tide when the moon is just below the crest...' Zoya looks at the heavens to get inspiration. 'Do you see the moon rising there, sir?' Paw-Claw looks at where Zoya points in the sky. 'As you note, sir, the moon is crested. I will be gone before it dips...'

'And you'll take your Remy with you?'

'Yes sir, I will take my Remy with me because I travel to Blighty. Where they pay six hundred for boxes like mine. In fact, that's the amount I hoped for, sir. I am sorry to have disturbed you but, *you are right*, it would make more profitable sense to take my boxes with me. Thanks for making my mind up for me. I wish you peaceful night. And I offer you my sincere wishes apologies for disturbing you with this trifling matter. Enjoy your stay in town. I bid you a fond *adieu*.' Zoya taps his forelock with his finger and backs off, without turning, to show the fat-man the respect he deserves. He withdraws three metres, then turns, ready to march into darkness.

'*Not so fast...*' shouts Paw-Claw. 'Where is your stash? If it's close to here, maybe I can carry out a quick visit and see for myself, right?'

Zoya turns, a giant smile on his face: 'Not far away at all, sir. My craft is moored on the jetty. My little warehouse, the place I keep the bottles, is alongside. Five minutes' walk from here, if not less. Will you come?'

'Yes, lead the way.'

If Rakhim follows, Zoya does not know, because he dares not look back. He whistles and hums as he heads towards the anchorage. He maintains a fast pace and bounces on his toes.

'Not so fast...' Paw-Claw complains. 'I'm not quick on my heels.'

'Many apologies,' Zoya says. He slows somewhat. He sees that the fat man sweats.

'It is very dark now,' states Paw-Claw. He looks about. 'Is it much further?'

'Can't you smell the brine?' asks Zoya. 'It is just a few metres. Then we will be at my wharf. I roped my craft along a jetty...'

'You never told me how you came by these bottles. Was there an associated tale?'

'Very much,' exclaims Zoya. He moves alongside the fat-man, so they might walk together. 'I salvaged the treasure from a *scupper*...'

'A scupper. What is that?'

'We had left Saint-Martin Boulogne, ten days since, when we saw sign of a craft in distress near Cap Blanc Nez. The ship had stopped, hammered, stuck in dangerous mud holes, near that point. A spiked outcrop of rock had pierced her hull. The cap-it-tan of the wounded vessel caught our attention, so we anchored alongside, although this was a perilous act. We took her passengers and stock off 'er with a boatswain's rope. Once we had saved all we could, their captain scuppered his vessel because the tide rose fast, and he was about to lose the lot anyway. He said at least his boat was underwritten, though not the cargo. He further told us he could not recompense my crew for our efforts but said payment might be anything we could fairly carry over to our small fishing craft in the abbreviated time allowed. Sir, we couldn't bring back much, since his crew and saved cargo filled most of our capacity, plus we came over by rope and so we had to hold on to the treasure as well as cling to the rope. Despite that, I clutched four rare boxes of XO. Later the skipper of the scuppered craft approved of my choice and said it was a fair reward for a gallant rescue of men and freight.'

Paw-Claw looked impressed by the tale, so Zoya embellished it further by adding: 'Monsieur, we watched that wounded watercraft descend into cold and frothy waves. I don't mind admitting I shed a tear as she sunk into darkness. But we had saved her crew, and her cargo, and that was surely a noble deed. We offered a prayer of thanks as she slipped beneath the brine.'

'So these bottles have sentimental associations for you? Are you sure you want to separate yourself from them?'

'Oh *yes*, sir. I know these bottles mean a lot to me, but space on a fishing boat is a scanty commodity. I am sure you understand. Also, I will never touch strong liquor, to be honest. And so, for these reasons, I prefer these high-quality products go to a connoisseur of the utmost esteem.'

'Of course,' says Paw-Claw. They arrive at the entrance to the port.

Zoya checks behind him, once. He wants to see if Rakhim is keeps close. He glimpses a darting shadow. He assumes it must be his pal.

'Not long now,' Zoya says. 'My craft is at the end. That is where my lock-up is...'

'Good. I am getting anxious. This place is lonely. Is there nobody about?'

'Security guards up there...' Zoya points to a shipping container on stilts. The place he points out is a makeshift office with steamed-up windows and faded interior lights. 'They have cameras all over. You are quite safe.'

'Good,' says Paw-Claw. He pulls the collar of his grandad-shirt open. Zoya guesses he must be feeling clammy.

'There she is,' Zoya announces. He gives a sincere smile. 'That's the fishing boat. A beauty, isn't she?'

'Yes, I guess,' says Paw-Claw. He looks around. He seems a good deal more uneasy now that he approaches the end of the pier. The podgy man gazes into the inky black water. 'One boat looks like another,' he admits.

'Yes,' agrees Zoya. 'That's because you are a clumsy, land-lubbing tub of lard, aren't you?'

'What?' says the man. His piggy eyes go wild. 'What did you call me?'

'I said you were a fat sweaty pig. A filthy *gros cochon en sueur*...'

'How dare you...' says Paw-Claw. 'Take that insult back or our deal is off.'

'You dirty animal *en peluche à fond gras*...' Zoya grabs the large man by his sweating wrist. 'Before you get loose like a goose, I need *that*...' he claws at the man's expensive watch.

'They will lock you in the Bastille for this outrage... you are nothing more than a pirate...get off of me, you disgusting beast.'

'Pirate am I?' says Zoya. 'You don't know the half of it!' He head-butts the man. Zoya hears splinters of bone. Paw-Claw falters, perilously close to the water. He holds his face in pain. Blood oozes from his nostril. That is when the shadow moves. It's Rakhim. He proceeds with deadly speed. Zoya sees, at a glance, the shiny steel hammer-head being wielded. The blunt toughness thuds into the fat-man's greasy temple. Paw-Claw doesn't collapse, like they might expect, but instead he looks at this *new* attacker with astonished eyes. He attempts to utter *something*. Rakhim strikes him again, this time with double the force. He swings the hammer from his shoulder and hits the man between the eyes.

Paw-Claw staggers, splutters, then stumbles. He tumbles, face forwards, into the dead-dark waters with a distinctive *splosh!* The sound of his bellyflop echoes around the harbour walls. The noise rouses the seabirds.

'Dammit you *hemar*, I wanted that watch... you did not give me time to grab it...' Zoya says.

'Oh well,' Rakhim answers. He wipes his hand on a sleeve and fixes the murder-weapon back into his waistband. 'Job done.'

'Is it justified to discard human life in such a beastly manner?' Zoya asks. He opens the door of his lock-up hut, searching for a long-handled billhook. He takes a long sniff of the air that feels stale inside the confined space.

'You saw how the domesticated pig was, what a gluttonous animal he'd become, with rolls of fat and tiny eyes... oinking and squealing. That beast was ripe for the killing floor. We did the world a flavour,' explains Rakhim.

Zoya cannot find his billhook but brings out a metal fuel-can and a pair of bolt cutters. 'Are you going to help me with this?'

His companion nods.

'Good. I have to borrow a pair of oars. I know where some are put away, over there, but they need to be cut down from a rack...' Zoya holds up his cutters. Then he points at a boathouse. 'Also, I need fuel...' He turns his back to locate a length of hose from the hut.

'What does it matter, anyway?' Rakhim asks, coming close. 'About the pig, I mean. You're planning your escape, right? So what does it matter?'

Zoya stiffens his posture and turns his neck. He raises an eyebrow. 'What do you mean?'

'I think you are going tonight. Am I right? I do not think you have to wait for the tide, do you? You have a boat, you're an adequate sailor, and the world is your lobster, yes? I'm not stupid... I know you don't need an oar for a motorized boat. So, it seems, you plan a stealthy departure. I guess it will be tonight.'

'You're barking through the wrong door,' Zoya replies. 'I'm preparing things for my next trip for the Lady Marquesse. You've got me all wrong...'

'Have I? Why do you have to steal fuel if it's for the Lady Marquesse'? Why not ask her for an advance on what's owed?'

'I am just gonna transfer fuel from one vessel to another...' Zoya replies, attempting to deal with his pal's doubt. 'It's a common thing. We do it all the time.' He moves to a set of ramshackle steps. These lead to a low craft, hitched water-height, and lashed to a fishing vessel: CH 31134. He pulls away a heavy tarpaulin to expose a six-man rib. Orange light glimmers on the wrinkled slops of black water. Zoya treads onto the smaller boat to consider what he has got. Rakhim gazes out to sea and distinguishes a row of buoys that mark out the navigation channel. In the middle distance, he sees the sea-wall that shields the harbour approach. He watches as Zoya opens the fuel tank on the main fishing vessel. He gazes as Zoya sucks one end of the hose, then pushes the squirting end into his jerry-can.

'You want me to get those oars? Rakhim offers.

'That would help. Do you know where I pointed?'

'Yeah, there's a festoon of flaglets... I guess that's where the oars are tethered...'

'That's right, you got it... thanks.'

Rakhim takes the heavy-duty bolt-cutters with him. As he goes, he mutters: 'This is going to cost you much more than fifty euros...'

'I guessed such...' Zoya responds. He looks up and gives his pal a grin.

∽

A little later, Rakhim returns, dragging two cumbersome, sapphire-tinted oars with him. He leaves them by the wall and observes Zoya as he completes his inspection of the outboard motor on the rib. Zoya looks up and says, 'We need to get a barrel from my shed...'

'Okeley dokely.'

Zoya treads up from the landing pontoon, then joins Rakhim by the lock-up. 'It is very heavy, I am afraid. We will need to roll it to the edge. Then I can rope it before we low-er it into the rib...' Zoya pulls a hefty length of rope from his hut, then clears away a twist of fishing nets, to get at the barrel. It's difficult to see in the dim light, but Rakhim squints to assess the big oak container that Zoya expects him to manage.

'Sheesh,' he says. 'It is mighty big. Can it be done?'

'I got it here alone. But it will take two to lower, which is why I need your hands.' With these words, Zoya squeezes behind the cask, and he heaves. It's a confined space. He doesn't have much elbow room: 'I need help...' he says, offering a grimace.

'Oh, sorry, *yes*.' Rakhim pulls the top part while Zoya pushes the bottom.

After effort, they get the upright keg into the open air. 'That's the hard part done,' Zoya says. He licks his lips and stretches his arms. Meanwhile, Rakhim inspects his fingertips for splinters. 'If we can slant the butt on its side, we might be able to tip it over. Then it will be easier to roll it to the edge. It will take a big effort to topple, though, to bring it down. But if we lean on one side, I think we can topple it over. We will *both* need to heave.'

Rakhim pushes his warm muscles solid against Zoya's arms. They prepare to tip the barrel. 'Should you count?' Rakhim asks with a chuckle.

'Good idea. After three: One, two, and *three*.'

The first hump is not enough. But at least they know how much muscle will be required to tip the object. They prepare for another try. 'Ready? One-two, and three.' This time they bulldoze themselves into the it and it wobbles, then teeters on its lip for a moment, then the barrel overturns with a loud *crack*.

'Excellent,' Zoya says with a smile. However, he looks anxiously at the security hut. Luckily, there is no sign of anyone moving around. So he supposes the sleepy security guys didn't hear the noise. Zoya rubs his hands on his pants.

Rakhim gazes at the barrel. 'That's a monster. Why do you want it on your boat? Won't it compromise your escape? '

Zoya looks at his friend with narrowing eyes. He draws a breath: 'Yes, it will slow things, but I have to throw it overboard when I'm in the waves, do you see?'

'Right, so this big heavy thing we lugged so hard is to be thrown in the brine. What is in it that can be so precious yet so disposable?'

'Bo Runner...'

Zoya thinks he hears a faint gasp from Rakhim. In the dim glow of the harbour lights, he sees fresh astonishment on his pal's face. 'What did you say?' Rakhim asks.

'I think you heard me — it's Bo Runner what's in the barrel. That's why that thing is heavy.' Rakhim gives the container a longer stare. It's as if he's mulling the news in his mind. Zoya gives his pal a moment to deal with it, then he says: 'Come on, help me get this bloody thing to the edge wall. We need to get our backs onto it.'

'How come he does not smell?' Rakhim asks, before he bends to push the barrel.

'What, him inside the keg?'

'He's been there for days.'

'This is a pickling barrel. Special thing. Designed to contain liquids and sloppy fish. It is watertight and sealed. I put vinegar in before I hammered the lid and tarred the top. I pickled the guy like a herring.'

'My zarumba,' Rakhim exclaims. 'How did Bo Runner get into it?'

Zoya looks at his pal. He shakes his head and gives a soppy grin: 'I put him in there, of course.'

Rakhim grunts and then puts his back into the work. The drum makes a crunchy noise as they push it. It rolls quite well. Soon they have to stop again. 'I have to rope it and then comes the tricky part,' announces Zoya. 'We must lower it halfway into the rib, then drop it the remainder...'

'Since I am helping you with this exertion, would you mind telling me what happened?'

Zoya smiles. His teeth gleam in the faint amber light: 'Do you want to know why I put Bo Runner into this pickling-barrel? Is that what you are asking?'

Rakhim shakes his head. 'I understand why you did it. You needed to preserve him until you disposed of the body. What I don't get is why didn't you fling the body into the brine when you had the chance? It would have been easier...'

'Oh, I didn't do this to him at sea. I needed Bo Runner back at port...'

Rakhim frowns. He pops his knuckles. 'What for?'

'I needed help to bring the craft in. It is a two-man job, do you see?'

'So you slaughtered him on the jetty? *Here* where we stand?'

Zoya nods to his pal in the amber light. 'I slit his passage with a gullet-knife once we were landed.'

'You put him in the barrel?'

'Yep, I squeezed him into the fish barrel. Next morning I added the vinegar. I tarred the thing over. Job done.'

'Why did he deserve such a terrible fate?'

'He came careless and lazy. Flaky and unreliable. The worst thing...'

'Yes?'

'He started to get cold fleet about the drop-offs. He told me he was getting second-hand thoughts about casting the regular load adrift beyond Point Blanc.'

'What was the regular load?'

Zoya grabs an end of rope and begins knotting it into an improvised harness, so they can lower the barrel. 'Each trip we took six exiles with us. We cast them adrift into the brine before we reached the Jersey listening station...'

'Refugees?'

'Yes, it was a good operation. Worked as sweet as a honey clock, but guess what?'

'What?'

'Bo Runner had feelings of extreme nervousness about it... he was getting cold fleet.'

'The jitterbugs?'

'Exactly. So he made it known it would be our last trip. Bo Runner told me to go to the wheelhouse to stabilize the boat when we approached Point Blanc, but I knew that was an excuse because he wanted me out of the way. He lifted the tarpaulin from where we hid the refugees and took out a woman and her child... I spied this from my position.'

'My zarumba,' Rakhim says.

'I watched what he did. He put four men adrift in the inflatable toy-boat and they wobbled away in the brine, happy harry. But Bo Runner finds his own life vest out and straps it around the woman, under her pits. He has also somehow gets a tiny floating vest for her infant. I think he made it out of polystyrene. So he puts these life jackies around them and tapes them. Then lowers them real careful into a separate lilo and watches them paddle into the night. Afterwards, when they're out of sight, he comes to find me. Bo Runner says: 'I am glad you didn't witness. Pitiful. I won't be doing it no more. Not never again. I will tell the Lady Marquesse to stuff her shit when we get back to land. It is disgraceful. I do not want to do this shit no more... that's what I will tell her..."

'He didn't mind casting the men adrift? But had pangs about depositing the mother and child?'

'Exactly. I suppose he could see this was just the beginning of how things would be. Soon there would be a steady stream of women and children...'

'So you cut his throat before he could say shit to the Marquesse?'

'Naturally. Wouldn't you? And don't forget he cast that woman adrift wearing *his* life vest. So I knew he had no intention of ever going back to sea. Plus, imagine if that woman somehow survived her ordeal. What if she told her tale? She might describe us. She might even recall the number of the boat that took her. I had to deal with that possibility, didn't I? Strictly a business decision, by the way. I didn't dislike Bo Runner at all. He was a good skipper. But I had to protect my income, didn't I? My future was at stakes.'

'Obviously, I see that.'

'So I hammered Bo Runner into this cask. And here we are.'

Rakhim nods and sighs but says nothing.

'Can you me help lower it into the rib?'

Rakhim moves around and pulls one end of the rope. He looks over at Zoya, 'Do you carry that gullet-knife with you all times?'

'Me? Just when I am on board. Why?'

'Because I carry my hammer everywhere.'

'Yeah, I noticed.'

'You never know when you might need a weapon. You ought to keep your knife close-by, just saying...'

'Thanks for the advice.'

Zoya lashes his end of the rope around one part of the barrel, then rolls the heavy tub back and forth, to take the strain. After this, he pushes his fingers out, to take the tip of Rakhim's end, but instead of feeling the braid of rope he expects, he touches his friend's hairy wrist. Abruptly, Rakhim pulls him off balance. His pal has the advantage because he's stood steady, legs wide, in a fighting stance. Zoya feels his elbow dragged. Soon, he is draped over the fish barrel.

'Are you ready to be flogged?' Rakhim asks. His lips uncomfortably close to Zoya's ear.

'What?' Zoya whispers. He feels a bony knee pushed between his thighs. Then he feels his pal's elbow jutted solidly into his spine. After this, he's dominated and prone... with his belly on the tub and his toes sliding on the cobbles. Rakhim secures Zoya into position by tethering his wrists to the tub and tying his ankle together, with shreds of netting taken from the fisher's hut. Once he's done, Rakhim takes the bolt croppers and wanders away. Zoya guesses he's going to the fishing boat. Zoya watches him with one eye but cannot move a muscle. When his pal returns, he is carrying a radio aerial that he bolt-cut from the top of the boat's wheelhouse. Rakhim tries it in the air. The makeshift whip makes an agreeable *crack*. Rakhim goes to Zoya and touches his cheek with the swishy tip of the aerial-crop. He leans in, to whisper: 'When did you guess?'

'Hew?'

'Don't say *hew*, it's not a word,' rebukes Rakhim. 'Speak English properly, or not at all. When did you figure I worked for the Marquesse? When did you realize I was Paw-Claw?'

'I did not know immediately,' Zoya admits. 'Things started to fall into place bit-by-bit. I decided I would take you with me in the rib. I planned to throw you into the brine, along with the pickle-barrel, when the time was ripe. What happens now? What will you do next?'

'The lady says *you must be punished*. So, you will be flogged. That is how they deal with mutineers, right?'

'Actually, they hang them...' Zoya suggests.

'Ah, yes, *they do*. That comes later."

12

Eimear paces the hall carpet with baby Amira. She inspects her chewed fingertips, and she sighs. At five-and-twenty past four, the doorbell rings. Eimear goes to the glass panel to see through the glass. She expects to see the outlines of two large police officers. But the shape is not big enough. There is only one blurry silhouette, and it's small. She opens the door to see through the crack. It is Arnie.

'Hi, honey, it's me,' says Nigel's girlfriend.

'Oh hello! I did not expect *you*. It might be best if you came straight indoors.' Eimear opens up but looks along the street with curious eyes. Before closing the door, Eimear notices a strange car outside, a small hatchback. There's nobody in it. She thinks it must belong to Arnie.

Arnie enters the old man's house. It is clear the girl has been crying. Her face is blotchy red, her makeup depleted. 'What's the matter, love?' Eimear says, as she rubs Arnie's shoulder.

'It's *him*. Nigel. We had a big row... I did not know where to go or who to tell.' Arnie looks at little baby Amira and she says: 'Hello sweet thing... can you imagine? We had the most horrible dispute about *this* innocent angel.'

'You'd better come into the main room and explain.'

The girls stroll to the lounge. Eimear invites Arnie to sit. 'I'd like to offer you tea and hospitality,' she says. But to be honest, I'm in a state of sixes and sevens myself. I feel confused by recent events. I hope you don't think I'm being unpleasant or unfriendly, but I'm in a state of uncertainty at the moment.'

'You are?' Arnie asks.

'George got arrested. The peelers came. They hauled him away. In cuffs.'

'Oh my God. You must think I'm a complete blockhead,' says Arnie. 'Fancy me coming here with my insignificant problems when you have your own. Why was he arrested? '

'To be honest, that is the million-dollar question. I don't know for sure. It must be connected to this little one. The rozzers were terribly serious when they came. They clapped the old man into cuffs, and it took two giant Peelers to lead the poor fellah away...'

'Oh, good God. I'm genuinely shocked. So when does he get out? What happens next? Does he go to court or straight to jail? Shit! Sorry about my French, but Nigel will have to know about this news. It's *his* dad we are talking about, after all...'

'Yes, you are right. Where is Nigel? We need to tell him his dad is down the nick.'

'That is the thing. I don't know where he is. He stormed off in a terrible rage. He said he wouldn't be back. That's why I came here. I figured he might have come here. I tried calling, but he's switched his mobile phone off.'

'He couldn't have run off at a worse time...'

'Sorry, I'm really miserable.' Arnie cries again. Large salty dribbles streak plump cheeks. 'Nigel said I was forcing him into things...' she sobs. 'He said our relationship is going down the shithole, and, sorry, he blames *you*.'

'Me?' Eimear shudders. She stares at the baby.

'I'm sorry, I know it's not your fault, but it's a notion he's got into his thick head recently. This argument has been brewing for months... actually before he even met you. But this evening things boiled over.'

"Look, I'd love to talk about this, but as you can see, I'm in a bit of a pickle myself. Would you be able to help, perhaps?'

'Yes, love, anything. What do you need?'

'I have to go into work, to the residential care home. Clongowes, it's on the outskirts of town. I need to see Mrs. Soomro. She's the night manager. I need to catch her immediately, the moment she gets in. I need to explain the situation as best I can. I need to see if she would allow me a night off duty.'

'Can't you phone her?'

'Nope, that wouldn't work. I need to see her face-to-face to put across my case. I could get a Big Red Taxi to collect me, but I couldn't ask the cab driver to look after the baby, could I? And I'm not allowed to take the baby inside. And if Mrs. Soomro says *no*, what would I do next? Do you see? I'm in a right jam.'

'Do you want me to take you? If I drive you there, I can look after the baby while you are explaining things to the boss-lady?' Arnie gazes across with big blotchy eyes. 'And if she says *no*, I can look after the baby until you come back out.'

'Would you do that?'

'Of course, it would be a pleasure. Plus, it would give us an opportunity to chat about the pickle I'm in. It will take my mind off problems. It is the best solution for both of us, don't you think?'

'It would be perfect if you could do it. Are you sure I would not be taking advantage of your good nature?'

'No, of course you wouldn't.' Arnie brightens. She rubs away her tears with the tip of a fleshy thumb. 'It is the tonic I needed. I am feeling better already.'

'Don't say that...'

'No, I'm serious. You are almost a sister to me. Do you need to prepare the baby?'

'Yes, I do,' says Eimear. She bites her lip because she's aware of the time. 'Frankly, I have to get on with things — I'm sorry but I can't stop and yack...'

'Can I help? Can I help get the baby ready?'

'That would be lovely. Wouldn't it Amira?'

The infant chortles.

The girls chat about Nigel on the journey to the Clongowes house in Arnie's cheerful hatchback. Eimear holds the child in her arms. She sits on the back seat because there is no cradle or special child-carrier for little baby Amira. The traffic is light, and the trip is short. Soon they arrive at the cramped parking lot adjacent to the residential home.

'It's good of you to do this charity for me,' says Eimear. 'And it's nice of you to offer to hold the baby while I explain things to Mrs. Soomro.' She checks the dashboard clock and sees there's just four minutes before her shift starts.

'It's been a pleasure. I'm glad I could assist. Thanks for helping me stop thinking about things with Nigel,' says Arnie. She offers a pleasant smile. 'I'm going to be your sister one day, I'm sure of it. I will take proper care of the little one while you are off doing your thing Do not worry.'

'Thank you, love, I will not be long, just a few minutes... I hope.'

Eimear unstraps herself from the rear seat and climbs around. She promptly passes the baby girl into Arnie's arms. They had earlier wrapped the infant in fresh clothes, and she smells sweet. Arnie takes the child with a tender nod.

Eimear trots into Clongowes via the side staff-entrance.

Inside the care home, Eimear immediately traces the night manager. She is not at her desk, but instead she's supervising relatives who came to see a resident taken ill during the afternoon. 'You're late,' she says with a frown.

'I'm sorry, Ms. Soomro, my, er, well, a family member got arrested, you understand?'

'Right,' says the supervisor, with a raised eyebrow. 'And?'

'So I was left alone to take care of the baby...'

'What baby?'

'Um, well, the little one who belongs to the family member that got arrested. My, she is a lovely little girl, too. A singular peach. Sweet as sweet can be.'

'Yes, that's all very well, but I need to see you in your uniform very quickly... so come help me. You know this is the busy time of the evening... and you are a few minutes late *already*.'

'Well, the thing is, Missus, I *cannot* you see...'

'Cannot? What do you mean you can't?'

'My, uh, my family member has not yet returned from the cop-shop. So I am *actually* left holding the baby...'

'If that is the case, then where is this baby now?' Mrs. Soomro tilts her head and throws Eimear an accusative look.

'Um, sorry Missus, the babe is outside, in a friend's car, parked in the staff car park...'

'Who is this friend in the car? Is it your boyfriend, by any chance?'

'Er, no. Not at all, actually. The car belongs to a girl of my acquaintance who agreed to bring me here. She's a kind-of a half-sister to me, *sort of...*'

'Well, go tell your half-sister that she can take care of the baby tonight. Because we are busy here. And if this is your way of asking for a night off work, it simply won't do, young lady. This is *not* the way to go about things...'

'I'm sorry, but if you saw the baby, I'm sure you would appreciate my predicament. She's a little angel, so she is. And maybe my, uh, family member will be discharged from the cop-shop at ten o'clock. That is what the Peelers said when they hauled him away. Then I could come into work, say at eleven, to complete the rest of my shift. I will make up the hours, I promise. Please, missus, I beg you... I don't normally ask for favours... this is an isolated case. I am not even asking for myself, do you see? I am in a terrible fix... I wouldn't beg you like this unless it was serious.'

'Hmm,' Mrs. Soomro taps a finger against her bottom lip. 'Maybe I can allow you two hours. Nothing more, though. Just until your, er, family-member gets released from custody. Be back here by midnight. Do you agree with that? I will finish things here, then I will come to see this baby of yours. Yeah? So wait in the car-park for me. And do not fly-off until I have seen this young one you are telling me about...'

'Oh, thank you, Mrs. Soomro. You do not know how much you have helped. I will repay you a thousand-fold for this kind-heartedness.'

'You had better.'

Eimear dashes from the side-door of Clongowes' house to tell Arnie that her manager is coming out to see baby Amira. She feels a slight flutter in her belly and a lovely free-floating sensation... it's as if a guardian angel had lifted all her recent problems from her shoulders.

But when she gets to the car park, there is no sign of that small, bright hatchback. There is no sign of Arnie. No sign of her car.

Eimear's eyes widen and she scratches her jaw. 'Where did she get to?' Maybe she's moving the car around. Sometimes drivers do that sort of thing, to keep an engine running or find a better place to park. But the staff car-park remains half empty and there was no better place to park than the bay they had already found. There is no sight or sound of any car nearby. Eimear listens to the background noises, to some dog barks, to the wind in the leaves, to a burger wrapper that rustles in the bramble. She cannot detect the sound of a car engine running.

Eimear waits calmly beside a plant-pot for Arnie's car to return. She reasons that Arnie went to get a cuddly toy for the baby. That is the most reasonable explanation. *Yes, that must be it.* She will be back in a moment.

Ten minutes pass and Eimear feels a rolling sensation in her stomach. It's like she is about to be sick. She swallows, wipes sweat from her forehead, and notices a sour taste in the back of her mouth. She hears heavy clomping footsteps approaching from the side door.

She guesses its Mrs. Soomro. Her supervisor had come out to see the baby.

Eimear scratches against her cheek with her bitten nails.

'Well, where is she?' Mrs. Soomro says. The supervisor stands next to Eimear. Her arms are crossed. The woman scans the empty car-park. She makes a low guttural noise that almost becomes a growl.

Eimear gazes at the ground and breathes deeply. Her knees tremble. She cannot answer.

'I said where is she? Where is this baby of yours? This baby you were so keen to show me?'

Eimear swallows a bubble of saliva after it forms in her mouth. She opens her lips to say something... but no words come out.

'Good heavens, young lady. You have ushered me out for nothing. Nothing at all. I cannot deal with this type of nonsense at the moment. I have too many things happening. You should know I am extremely disappointed in you... you ought to feel ashamed of yourself. You must be feeling very silly. Go off and do whatever you have planned, then come back at midnight. We will have a word about this prank when I feel less angry! But, for now, be off with you... go on, *go*.'

Mrs. Soomro turns. Her arms remain crossed over her chest. She has a bitter look on her face.

Eimear rubs her elbow and crosses the parking area. She heads for the exit. Her neck is bent, her shoulders sag and she senses wooziness in her head.

It takes forty minutes to get back to George's house on foot.

She gets the key to the door from her bra. Then she plods, with a sense of determination, up the red-tile garden path. She hoped-against-hope that Arnie had mixed up their agreed plan and had erroneously returned home with the baby. But the car's not on the road outside. There is no sign of Arnie.

Eimear unlocks the door and kicks off her pumps in the hall. 'Oh

Jesus, Mary, and Joseph... what am I to do?' Then she hears a clatter from the back of the house. Her pulse races. She stands stock-still, not daring to move a single hair. *Who is it?* Her muscles tense, her eyes widen. She struggles to control her breathing. If it's Nigel, he's inclined to do something extreme, perhaps violent. 'Oh Mary, Mother of God, I hope it is not *him...*'

She picks up another *thud*. This time it's as if someone is smashing into an object, then replacing it. *Burglars?* Then she hears shambling footsteps. The footsteps head *her way*.

Eimear's eyes widen. Her lips go dry. She watches a figure approach.

'Ah it is you, miss. I heard someone clanking around...'

Eimear feels an overwhelming sense of relief when she sees its only George. With a voice that becomes strangled by tears, she says: 'It's you, thank Jesus. My God, what a time I've had. I think I'm in a nightmare. I had a dreadful time when you were in the cop shop.' Her knees sag. Eimear hyperventilates. Her eyes overflow with exhausted tears. She rocks back and forth on her heels before crumpling to the floor.

A little later, she comes around. She is in the lounge. Her body is laid on the floor, face up. Her feet are on a cushion. George sits close. He looks tenderly her way. 'Oi has a glass of fresh orange juice for you, young miss.'

Eimear gives the old man a muzzy smile. She tries to raise her head, but it won't move readily. George comes around to her side and pushes her shoulders to slide an extra pillow under her neck. 'That will yelp you until yee can stand properly.'

'What happened?' she mumbles.

'Y'fainted, miss, that is all. When y'ready, take a drink of the orange.'

'I'm sorry,' she says.

Eimear collects herself bit-by-bit. She raises her head a bare inch. She moves her elbows, and she pushes up until she sits with her back rested on the side of his wing chair. The old man crouches to pass her the orange drink. 'Yawl drink this yup, because it will strengthen yee.'

She does what he says. She promptly feels better. Then she recalls the terrible thing that happened and the awful crunch in her stomach triggers again. 'Oh my, *oh my...* make it go away, George. Make the pain go away...' Her tears fall. 'Oh my God George... I do not know how to tell you...'

'Where is the baby?' the old man asks. For the first time, she recognizes he is unsettled. His eyes narrow, his hands are tight. He holds his breath.

'She took it...' Eimear whispers.

'Who? Who took the baby? Did social services get yer? Where is y'baby now?'

Eimear shakes her head. 'Nigel's girlfriend, Arnie, took her. They planned it. It is a plot. They grabbed her. George, they snatched our baby.'

'Hell,' says George.

After drinking the rest of her juice and sitting easily in the armchair, it strikes Eimear she had not asked George about his day at the cop-shop.

'So, George, what was it all about? Why did the Peelers drag you in?'

'Theft...' he confides. He presents a sad expression.

'Theft?' she asks. Her voice sounds sharp. It was the *last* thing she thought he would say. 'What bloody theft? What have you been thieving, George? I thought they got you for concealing the babe. I thought something more serious... You were doing shoplifting too, were you, you old goat?'

'No, nothing,' he tells her. 'I yam innocent...'

'But the officers took it seriously, didn't they? Clapping you in irons and taking you off for hours. What did they accuse you of doing?'

'Like I said, it was theft. I didn't steal any kind of thing in my life ever, and certainly not the bike...'

'What bike?'

'They said I stole the bike off the paperboy y'other week...'

'But that's absurd.'

'The boy's parents filed a complaint...'

'Well, of course you did not steal the bicycle. In fact, you kept it safe for him. You even fixed it up. Mary, mother of God, you even painted it...'

'That's the mess. They say it's the very definition of theft. I treated the bike as if my own. I should not have painted her up... that was where I went wrong on y'it.'

'Well, I hope you told them the truth, George. I hope you told them you fixed the bike, and you kept it safe for the boy until he was ready to collect it...'

'I told them it was an honest misunderstanding. They are going to charge me. Because I painted 'yer up.'

'Charge you?' Eimear shouts, 'With theft? This is totally insane... Don't they have anything better to do?'

'I treated the property as my own, see? For example, lending it to you one time...'

'Lending it to me? Is that what all this is all about? Britain is awash with crime and all the Peelers can do is nab a kindly old man who fixed up an old bike for a boy and leant it to a girl for a ride to the shops. A bike that he rescued from the gutter. The world has gone crazy...'

'They said that borrowing and lending the bicycle amounts to theft...'

'But, but... you were holding onto it to give it back. Where is the sense in charging you? There was no dishonesty, was there? I am sure there is not a dishonest bone in your body, George. Didn't you tell them that?'

'Keeping it in my shop was dishonest. I should have left it on the road or token it back to the parents. Yat's what they told me. I was wrong.'

'Good grief...'

'Anyway, other things have since happened that overshadowed all that. Important things...'

'Oh yeah? I think I am filled to the brim with big surprises today... but go on, tell me more...'

'The Border Force ran into a woman who lost her baby at sea.'

'Really?' Eimear raises an eyebrow. She gently bites her lip. 'How did you come by that kind of information?'

'I yave been calling the intelligence branch of the Home Office every day.'

'Have you? And they told you this?'

'Y'woman yapped in a quizzing. Says she was dunked off St Helier.'

'Dunked?'

'Tipped in sea. With 'er nipper. The night before I found 'er.'

'Wow, so your assumption could be true after all? What happens next?'

'I'm going to see her.'

'The woman?'

'Yes, but I need to go clandestine like. This is a hole-and-corner show.'

'What the hell does that mean? Seriously, George, sometimes you lose me with your words. You honestly do.'

'It is hush-hush...' George explains. 'I need to see 'er under wraps because of my bail conditions'

'Bail conditions?'

'Established by the police. Not to leave home, not to leave town.'

'My God, they've really thrown the book at you...' she suggests.

'If I need you, I will write you with this...' George pulls out a band-new cheapo phone from his back pocket. He holds it up for her to see.

'Good heavens, George! Do you have a mobile? Welcome to the twenty-first century. '

'Pay as it goes. I got this to call you and vicey-verso. I will take your number; you will take mine.'

'Hush-hush?'

'Very hush-hush, young lady...'

So they exchange numbers and Eimear takes a deep breath. She looks into the old man's eyes. 'George, I figured out where she took the baby...'

'You did?'

'Yes, but I need travelling money. A decent pile. I have to take a long trip. There is a place called Cathedral Green in Collingwood. I found the place on Google.'

George takes a roll of fifties. He hands the entire roll to her. It was as if he expected her to ask for cash. So was ready with lots of it.

'It's in Axbridge,' she qualifies.

'Right you are.' George smiles and nods.

'There's one more thing in my mind that I need settled before I fetch the baby.'

'What is it?' George asks.

'The young reporter fellah. He said you have *done it before*. Y'know, you've helped a migrant. Have you George? Have you done it before?'

'You ever 'eard of the boat people?'

'Nope.' Eimear gives a blank expression.

'It was afore y'were born.'

'Was it?'

'There were these refugees boating-out from Vietnam right though the seventies. I didn't think nothing of it till '80. I was working on a platform in Indonesia, near a place called Galang. Boatloads of Viets overran our island. I telephoned my missus at y'weekend. She was alive back then. I told 'er about all y'orphans that arrived. 'Undreds of 'em. She said, can't we do sommit? She communicated with the Indonesian authorities. They contacted the refugee camp. They chosed a yorphan for me to bring back 'ome. My missus completed the paperwork. She was a treasure.'

'And the orphan you brought back was your daughter?'

'We adopted her official. We brought 'er up as English. Some folks have got a long memory round 'ere. I'd thought they'd y'all forgotten. They never liked her while she grew up. Made her life rotten. Once she was old enough, she wanted to go back to South Asia. I get it. Back to 'er roots. So she went on 'oliday. She never camed back. Married a nice fellah. Settled in South Asia.'

'What did Nigel think?'

'He's our biological son, a-course. We had 'im once I got back from Asia. We brought 'em up together as sibs. But he was resentful all the while. He didn't like yer either. I don't know why.'

'What did he do to her?'

'Nothing bad. He just shunned yer. I thought he'd be protective towards 'er, but he never was. He hated being the younger, I suppose. They do, don't they? The younger hates being the youngest. So Nigel was pleased when she upped and went...he's never thought once of keeping in touch with 'er.'

'Did he pressurise her to go?'

'Oh no! Well I don't think so...'

'Ok, so.'

13

After completing a half-shift at Clongowes Care Home, as agreed with her boss-lady, Eimear takes a Big Red Taxi out to the town of Axbridge.

She has her largest overnight bag with her, stuffed with her best things. Maybe she thinks she'll never return from this undertaking. Eimear also has a five-penny bag for additional items. Her phone is fully charged. She hides most of the fifties in her bra. The rest of the money-roll hides in her purse.

The morning sparkles as her cab drives beyond meadows and cattle farms, towards the rattlesnake configuration of the Avon Gorge. 'Long way out, madam, *big trip*. Are you doing something special?'

Eimear shakes her head. She does not mean to be rude, but she's not in the mood for small talk. She needs to prepare for a confrontation. She closes her eyes to rest a little before they arrive.

Closer to their destination, the cab-man taps coordinates into his sat-nav. Eimear holds her breath, expecting him to say his machine *cannot find the place*. But the guy smiles a gummy smile into the rear-view mirror, and he says, 'Just ten more minutes, love...'

Eimear nods appreciation. Not at the guy, but at the gifted machine that sits upon his dashboard.

They soon arrive at a pleasant village. It has a quaint duck-pond and tapered streets that lead to rows of joyfully coloured cottages. They whoosh through an empty High Street, and stop, without warning, in a whinnied-hiss of tyres. Eimear looks from her window and sees a large Cotswold stone mansion. The manor-house is set back from the main road. The building has a vast, well-cut lawn and an imposing drive. 'Do you want me to drive you up to the front door?' the cab-man asks. He selects reverse gear.

'No!' Eimear shouts. She needs her approach to be silent. 'Do you mind staying here? Is it okay if I leave my bag with you?'

'How long you gonna be love?' asks the man. He scratches his temple.

'Maybe a few minutes. No more than half-an-hour, for sure.'

The driver gives a pained expression. But knows that all he can do, otherwise, is to turn the car around and head back to the coast, without any passenger. She satisfies him by adding: 'I will pay for *this part* of the trip, plus a generous tip...and I will require your services after I have had my meeting. How does that sound?'

'Okay love. That is good of you. I have to tell you, though, that this was a long journey. It will cost one-twenty. I'm sorry, love. But this was well out-of-my-way.' The driver rubs the back of his neck with a sweating palm. He expects she will have difficulties with the steep payment. Eimear smells the underarm odour from where she sits.

'Not a problem...' Eimear says. She leans forward and hands the driver three fifty-pound notes. 'For your time and trouble thus far.'

'Hey gee! That's good of you... I did not think, erm...'

She smiles, 'Don't worry yourself. It is not a problem... though, do me a favour, will you?'

'What do you need?' asks the cab man. He checks the notes to be sure they are not counterfeit.

'Be here when I get back. Can you do that? It is all I ask...'

'Trust me,' he tells her. He's assured by the quality of the crisp notes. 'I will be here. You can count on it. You're the boss.'

'Yeah.'

Eimear closes the taxi's sliding door, gingerly as she can, and takes her carrier-bag with her. She scans the road for other vehicles. There are no cars. Most of the houses in the neighbourhood have enormously long driveways... they don't need to park on the road. She shrugs, then steps up the shingle towards the immense house.

Eimear knows that, behind her, the Big Red Taxi moves to a better position. After she sees it turn, she walks on the lawn because it sounds less crispy. 'I hope they do not have dogs,' she whispers. It would be most unlikely if they did, she thinks.

She reaches the magnificent timber-framed facade of a spacious dwelling but chooses the path to the right of the main entrance, avoiding a front porch and keeping her feet on the grass as much as possible. There is a gate at the side that is wrought iron and lattice. The lattice has a climbing rose that ambles nimbly across an upper arch. The gate has a chain around it, but it is unlocked. Eimear unravels the chain and moves beyond the gate and into the back-garden of the property. The hinges grate and rasp when she closes the gate, but she takes care it does not clatter.

Her progress startles a song-thrush as she tiptoes into the back-yard. The bird shoots up to make an alarm call. She considers a magnificent garden laid in front and takes a stepping-stone path that leads to a shady pergola that she sees in mid-distance, and that is dotted with variegated foliage. When she reaches that point, she looks towards the main house and checks for open doors or twitching curtains. Satisfied the occupants of the mansion have not yet risen, she walks on, this time toward the darling-looking Wendy-house that's in one corner.

Now she sneaks quieter than before because she wants to set up an element of surprise.

Eimear arrives at the front-door of the dwarfish house and is pleased to see it is free of cobwebs. There are recent tracks in dampish turf, and marks that lead to the front-step. She approaches the door, and, for a moment, she contemplates using the small silver bell on the corner; to tinkle awake the fairy-residents of the elvish place. But she decides against, because she doesn't know how far the noise of the bell will carry. Eimear doesn't want to alert anyone in the big house.

She unlatches the Wendy-house door, and as she does, she sees the name of the playhouse written on a hand-painted wooden sign under the eaves: 'Rosamund House.' Eimear pushes the tiny door, stealthy and silent, and she pushes her nose into the gloom like a cunning cat sniffing for a mouse.

Whoever is inside the fairy-tale cabin makes a small yelp — because they see a bright glimmer of light coming from the door space.

Eimear enters. She gets her eyes used to the spooky half-light.

Arnie slaps her fingers against her cheeks when Eimear enters through the door of the Wendy-house. She gasps and gives an incredulous look. 'What? How? How did you know?'

Eimear ignores her idiotic questions and goes immediately to the dolls-cot that she sees in the corner of the cob-webbed hut. She hears Arnie's inhalations as she peers into the toy rocking-cradle. She sees the infant. She takes Amira from the doll's crib and hugs her. The baby is warm to touch and, though bleary eyed, seems unharmed by her experience.

'How did you know? How did you know about this place? How did you guess I was here?' Arnie croaks.

'Where's Nigel?' Eimear snaps.

'Nigel? I do not know. I have not seen him. Isn't he with you? I have not seen him since the ruckus...'

'I am here to get the baby...'

'She is not yours...'

'That's not the point,' says Eimear with bluntness in her eyes. Eimear returns the baby to the toy cot and moves rapidly and decisively towards Arnie. She pulls her fist back, then throws a direct punch into the other girl's face — just below the nose. Arnie wells-up instantly and touches her fingers to her cheeks as if she wants to shield from the pain. Her knees sag. 'Ow, freak-frack,' she whimpers. 'That bloody hurt.'

'It was for scaring the Jesus out of me, you stupid, *stupid*, mischievous, cow. I should cut you for what you did to me... you made me lose face where I work. You gave me heart palpitations that sent me bonkers. And you shredded my nerves to pieces. But you ain't worth the prison-time, sweetheart. You are nothing but a hoity-toity bitch. *And* you're mental — you need help from a psychiatrist, not a battering from me.'

'What are you going to do?' sobs Arnie.

'I told you. I am getting the baby back.'

'You will not tell them, will you? Please, promise you won't tell anyone...'

'Tell who? Tell the police? You have done this before, haven't you? Is that why you went down the coast to live? Is this why you were you kicked out of high society? Is it because of your transgressions? Is that why you found that poor mug Nigel to shack up with? You've done this plenty of times before, haven't you?'

'Please, please...' sobs Arnie.

'Do you have prior convictions? You grab babies, don't you?' Eimear sniffs. She looks around the hut: 'You bring them here, don't you? You sad, broken, little woman. You always bring them here, don't you? This is where it started, isn't it? Was it with Rosamund? Was she the first? Was she the first real baby you snatched? She was, wasn't she? I get it now. She was never a dolly, was she? She was a real baby, and you brought her here. Yet another fib you told me... Rosamund was an actual child!'

'Please...'

'You can relax, honey. I will tell no one. But if I hear you put a finger on another child, I swear I will go straight to the police faster than you can say: rich, girl, spoiled. Do you hear me loud and clear?'

'Please...'

Eimear takes a baby wipe from her carrier-bag and throws it into

Arnie's face. 'Get yourself cleaned up. You have blood and snot every-where. And do not follow us neither. Stay here for ten minutes. Go the way you came-in, sneak through the side gate...don't make any noise.'

'Thanks...' says Arnie.

'Don't thank me... thank sweet Jesus that I restrained myself. I never want to see your stupid ugly face again, do you hear?'

'Oh yes, of course.'

Eimear pulls the baby-sling from the penny carrier and grabs the baby from the Wendy-house crib. She turns and leaves. Eimear hears low sobs behind her as she crosses the long lawn to the waiting taxi.

14

Owen Bockett stands by the desk of his administrative assistant, Miss Nathalie Astolat. He lingers. He reflects, once again, that the name Astolat doesn't sound very English. But then he reminds himself that the Home Office checked her out, and she has *no history of doubt*. But this was the third time his assistant returned late from lunch in a fortnight. Something had to be said.

He looks at the fresh photograph on her desk and leans closer, narrowing his eyes, to gaze at the image. The image shows Nathalie on the arm of a muscular and handsome man in his thirties. In the new photo she has two children, one aged around three who cuddles her arms, and a second, probably five, who holds her legs. Who are these people? Cousins? Neighbours? A stepbrother and offspring? The only information Owen Bockett knows for sure about Nathalie is that she is single. He reminds himself of her *résumé*: she arrived without credentials, no formal qualifications, very few skills, no work experience, virtually no accomplishments, and assuredly no ambitions. The only positives were that her birth certificate confirmed British citizenship, and she possessed a special type of inexplicable canniness that meant she presented herself well on her Civil Service selection day. The only other feature Owen remembered about her was that she told everyone she was 'single and lived with mom.' Today her trustworthiness was under suspicion, because it was the third time she'd been late back from lunch in a fortnight.

The twin doors swing open, and Nathalie Astolat saunters in. She makes a nonchalant beeline for her desk. 'Are you okay, Owen?' she asks. She throws her head back and runs her hands through the sides of her hair. Owen can see sweat stains under her arms.

Owen Bockett frowns because he hates his first name being used, especially by someone who is younger or subordinate. Young people are not deferential these days. 'I'd prefer to be addressed as Mister Bockett,' he suggests.

'Whatever. Woss up?' Nathalie kicks off cheap heels and swivels the work chair around, readying to sit.

'I think you're late back from lunch.'

'Am I?'

Her insouciance jiggers Owen. He mumbles something under his breath and re-shuffles his feet. 'It is twenty past the hour...' He glances at the office wall-clock, to check he's precise. 'It means you're twenty minutes *overdue.*'

'Does it?'

'Um, yes, and *furthermore—*'

Nathalie sticks a finger in the air to stop him. Her eyes widen as she pulls a mobile phone from her bra strap: 'Hi babe, yes, got it...' Nathalie gazes at Mr Bockett and says: ''Scuse, Owen. I have to take this call... it is private, d'ya see? One moment.' She stands, turns her back on her boss, walks towards the far end of the office space, then says: 'Sorry babe. The dirty old man was overhearing me here. Yeah, what were you saying? Yes, I know, you devil! I would *too.* You know *I would.* Yes, I can. Ha ha! You'd be astonished how far they can stretch back...' Nathalie's words grow fuzzy as she moves away.

Owen Bockett does not know if he should wait at her desk or return to his office. He rocks back and forth on his heels. He flinches when Nathalie spits a bawdy laugh that can be heard across the room. He mutters and improvises. He grabs a file-docket from her desk, flips the cover, scans the first page of the report, then rolls his shoulders. He makes a coughing sound, he rubs his chin with his thumb, then he pushes his nose with the knuckle on his right hand.

Nathalie Astolat completes her urgent call and returns to her desk. 'I had to get that. It was Matvey. What a pain in the bum! The plumber cannot get to us until the end of next week. That means we're without hot water for another six days... at least.'

'Who is Matvey? Is that the name of your mum's plumber?'

'What? Are you mental or summink? Ha! Why would he be a plumber if we wanted a plumber. Duh?'

'I don't understand,' says Owen.

'Matvey is my other half, isn't he?'

'Other half?'

'Didn't you see my picture? That's him, in the photo on my desk. I thought I saw you peeking when I came in. He is a looker, right?'

'Is the man in the photo your other half?' Owen blinks and rubs his chin. He gazes at the photo. The way she talks, the words she uses, even her pronunciations of frequently-used expressions, they place a great mental strain on him. Owen understands only *half* of what she's saying. 'If I may?' Owen picks up the photo. 'This man is Matvey. This man is your other half?'

'Go it in one, Sherlock. There's no shit on you today, is there?'

'I thought you told me you were *single*...'

'Think again! Not anymore! Shacked up with Matvey now. Ready-made family as well! We have two wonderful babies. I love being a mummy. And my children love me. I couldn't be happier. Pig in shit.'

'Shacked? Does that mean you are living with this man?'

'Course it does. I'm living with my man and caring for our babies. He has a nice new-build just a bus ride from here, with a garden, two beds. Convenient.'

'What does Matvey do?'

'Odds and shit. I'm not sure. He has fingers in various cakes, here and there.'

'Cakes? Is he a baker?'

'Are you for real? You are messing with me, yeah? Sometimes you do my frigging head in, Owen, did you know that? Ha ha! You sound as daft as a toothbrush, sometimes, you *really* do.'

'The last time we spoke, on the quarterly, just three months ago, you said you lived with your mother. You told me you were single.'

'I know, magic, ain't it? Who'd of thought I would be a mummy, with two angels? And a wife to a wonderful man like Matvey? And in such short time? Miracle, ain't it?'

'Are you married to Matvey?' asks Owen. He drums his fingers on the side of his head, hoping to understand things.

'Well, you know, more or less. I don't want to go into the bedroom arrangements, *ha ha!* But I think you can safely say we are hitched... Why? Is that a problem?' This is the first time Nathalie Astolat studies her boss since she got back from lunch. When she does, she gives a knifelike stare that feels as if she's skewering him through the soul.

'You must divulge your new address and reveal your partner's *full* details. That's expected,' he says.

'You are kidding, right? Is there a form to fill out or summink?'

'Yes, there are several forms.'

'What do you need to know? What shit?'

'Details of Matvey. Your new postal address.'

'Yeah, get the form over to me. I will take a look when I get a chance. Anyfink else?'

'Where is his wife?'

'What?'

'This Matvey? Where is his wife?'

'What you on about? I'm his wife, ain't I? Didn't I already told you that, Owen?'

'Whose are those kids in the picture?'

'Darlings, right? Mine, aren't they? My two angels. Who would have thought I'd be a mummy out of the box? Not even I would've guessed a year ago! I love being a mummy, though. Matvey says I am a natural.'

'Erm?' Owen rubs his knuckles against his cheeks. 'How did you meet Matvey?'

'Ha! At the Mantra, in Slough. Do you know it? No, course you don't. Anyway, they have an over-thirties night and my girls and I go there on a Thursday. See what we can hook up with, like. Free admission for girls under twenty, of course. So Matvey is there with some other guys, all single, and he bumps into me, and we get chatting and he buys me a drink and, well, one thing leads to another, kapow, I am *getting off* with him! A week later and I'm shacked up with him, in his crib, and we are making sweet magic. Good, huh?'

There is a long pause. Owen Bockett tries to process all this information. He runs his hand across the file on her desk. 'What is this case?' He refers to the file he opened when she was on her call.

'Just shit.'

'Run through it with me.'

'If you insist,' says Nathalie. 'Basically, there's an old fool in a seedy dung heap in the south who imagines a baby fell out of a migrant's inflatable. He suggests that, somehow, the thing survived. He says the baby's mom is *here*, at our centre. And this old goat wants to bring the baby to reunite it — is that the right word? Anyway, he wants to bring the baby so he can get it together with its mum.'

'Why is it, erm, why did you say it was shit?'

'Well, it is, isn't it? The old fellah is clearly off of his trolley. How does he know this stuff? Where is he getting his information? And why he is wasting everyone's time?'

'But what if the baby was real? What if the mother was really at our centre? Wouldn't it be nice to get them back together? And you were supposed to meet with this gentleman. Why didn't you do that? Why didn't you meet him?'

'Spose it's because I thought it was a pile of shit. Doesn't it seem a pile of crap to you?'

'Didn't this old man suggest he knew who the mother might be?'

'Yeah, he says he has an angle on it. But the whole thing is ridiculous. How could he know this shit, anyhow? He is just a crazy, mixed up, old codger.'

'Still, please do not throw this file away. Do what needs to be done and bring it to me.'

'Are you sure, Owen? Only, I was going to file it in cabinet number one!'

'Cabinet number one? What is that?'

'Ha ha! The bloody shredder. That's the name I gived the fracking office shredder, ha!'

Owen Bockett winces: 'No, don't do that! Keep the docket safe. Enter the file number in the registry, then bring the file to me.'

'Whatever you say, Owen. You're the boss.'

Owen Bockett enjoys a break from his daily chores. During his lunch period, he begins the Daily Mail crossword. He spoons ASDA's well-priced strawberry-flavoured yoghurt into the corners of his crooked, slippery mouth. At one point he considers cleaning the lens of his reading glasses with a lemon wet-wipe, though he doesn't.

Miss Nathalie Astolat, his administrative assistant, is in the next office. She is the one *last* remaining Civil Servant, other than him, left on the Harmondsworth site. She leafs through a free evening paper that is printed by the airport. It's an open secret she seeks another job. This despite Bockett's constant comments about public employees getting handsome pensions upon retirement. But Miss Nathalie Astolat isn't stupid, in spite of her lack of any formal qualifications. She knows the Civil Service pension is a trap. And since the UKBA transferred responsibility to Bellon, a French organisation, everyone knew that all the original 'civvies' will someday get replaced by agency staff on short contracts. Miss Nathalie Astolat has made it known she thinks the entire Civil Service will be gone in five years.

Owen Bockett looks up from his puzzle to see his administrative assistant peering through the glazed slot in his screen door. She watches as he brings the plastic spoon to his crooked mouth. She watches him lick cream from its tip. She stares when he clicks his Home Office pen. She gazes at him, open-mouthed.

Owen Bockett returns to his crossword. Four across: thirty days and a summer girl's name, four letters. Bockett prefers four-letter names. He prefers names such as Owen, John, Mike, and Pete. He thinks people with four-letter names would make the world a safer place. His favourite town in the entire world is Deal. Four letters. It is where he spends a week each August. A week's break at Edna Leaf's bungalow-based B&B. Owen and his mother vacationed in four-letter Deal for thirty years. That was when she was alive, of course. He still took her now, *even so*. Every summer he places her casket on the window ledge at Edna Leaf's guest bedroom so mother can take the seaside air or see the view across the street. Owen Bockett liked the four-letter sound of Hove too. But hadn't taken mother there *yet*.

Owen lives in a five-letter town, Brent. One hour and fourteen minutes (sometimes one hour seventeen minutes) by bus and train. He disembarks at Heathrow Central. A shuttle bus takes him to Colnbrook. The shuttle bus is driven by an ethnic looking person whose name has several letters. At his workplace, the man at the security desk, a man who has a wispy moustache, flashes a name tag that reads: Seif. Yes, four letters! But when Owen researched *that* name, he found it meant *sword*. And Owen Bockett is not sure about a man whose name means *sword*. He thinks a man who has dark eyes, golden molasses skin, and is called *sword*, cannot be entirely trusted. Each morning, Owen gives the security man a nervous nod. He hopes his nod does not draw *sword's* attention.

After the puzzle, I'll look up Nathalie's name, Owen tells himself. He glances through the glass slit in his slatted door and meets his assistant's eyes. She is looking hard *his way*. Why? Did she want something? He sets down his pen and motions two bent fingers, gesturing her to come in. She hurries into his room.

'Did you need anything?' he asks.

'I must get away early, Owen,' Nathalie Astolat says. 'The plumber can come after another job. I must be home to let him in.'

'Today?' he asks.

'Of course, today. *Duh.*'

'Who takes care of the children while you are here?' asks Owen Bockett.

'What?'

'The children in the photograph on your desk?'

'My babies? Oh. yeah, right. My angels are in childcare, ain't they?'

'I don't know.' Owen shrugs. 'Are they?'

'What's that gotta do with me getting off early? Just asking...'

'I was simply thinking that if your mother, or maybe an in-law, had been looking after your children, perhaps one of those persons might open the door for the plumber.'

'Persons? Sometimes you don't half talk funny! My mum is not a persons! Ha ha! But is that your way of saying I can't get away early? Because, like I said, I genuinely need to shoot, like. And I mean *shoot* as in the next half hour, yeah? So can I get going *now*, Owen? Only I need to get myself moving, *pronto* like, as in *right now*.'

Owen Bockett knows, at this stage, he has the upper hand. He is also aware he won't hold onto the upper hand for very much longer. He knows she'll leave early whether he gives permission, *or not.* So Owen shapes his next question with care: 'Do your in-laws live nearby? I know they cannot help today, too busy I guess, but it must give you great peace of mind to know they're just a phone call away and so close they can pop over, any time, to help...'

'Um?'

'Where are your in-laws based?'

Miss Nathalie Astolat shakes her head madly as if she's trying to free a wasp that has become trapped in the twists of her hair. 'What are you talking about, Owen? You are not making sense. What do you mean in-laws? What does in-laws have to do with anything?'

'Just a simple question about your husband's parents. Where do they reside?'

'What does this have to do with the price of nuts?'

'Do you know? Do you know where Matvey's parents live?'

'Of course I know.'

'So where?'

Nathalie Astolat shrugs. She belches. After a long burp, she presents an angry stare. She doesn't offer an answer.

Owen continues: 'Where is your husband? Can't Matvey come and open for the plumber?'

'To hell with this, pal. Can I go right now? Or can't I?'

'I'm just being polite.'

'Well, it doesn't look sound like you are being frickin' polite. It sounds like you're being a frickin' idiot. I don't know what I did to deserve this in-terry-frickin' irrigation!'

Owen Bockett refrains from his natural propensity to apologise; though he finds it *painful* to hold the apology in. Ordinarily, in these circumstances, especially if someone is becoming unreasonable *with him*, his natural defence is to offer them a humble apology. That typically placates *them*. But not this time. This time, he knows, he must be firm: 'Can't your mother come and open for the plumber?'

'No, she cannot,' barks Nathalie. 'And you're being a shithouse for suggesting such a thing. Just say *yes*, so I can get going, you scungy old tosser.'

'I will overlook your impudence this time, because clearly you're under pressure, and *yes*, I will allow you to leave early, so long as you bring me that file.'

'File? What file?' shouts Nathalie Astolat. Her spittle strafes his National Health lenses.

'The old man that wants to bring the baby to its mother.'

'Oh, that shit. Yep. Right. Wait. It's coming.'

Miss Nathalie Astolat growls, spins on a toe, and exits his office in a flounce. She returns with glaringness splotched all across her face. She spins the file onto his pile of papers, where it bounces. As the docket jumps, it pushes his yoghurt over the tipping-point of his desk. The pot falls, rim side down, onto the zipper of Owen's trousers. It leaves a disgusting, white cream, stain.

Owen Bockett regards the stain upon his crotch, then he acknowledges the docket on his desk. He allows the meagerest of smiles. *He has her now.* He has the smug bitch exactly where he wants her. 'We'll talk about this tomorrow,' he declares. 'I should warn you it's a discipline matter.'

'Whatever,' mutters Nathalie Astolat. She parades out. She grabs her coat from the peg and departs the office. She slams the door as she leaves.

Owen Bockett rubs the cream into his crotch with the edge of his thumb. He enjoys the friction. He rubs harder. He keeps rubbing. Then he stops. He looks back at the crossword. Four across: Thirty days and a summer girl's name, four letters.

A little after three, Owen Bockett makes an external call. He logs the out-call in the official 'call history' book.

'Ah hello. My name is Bockett. I'm from Her Majesty's Immigration Service. I'm trying to get hold of a mister Florn. It's a mister George Florn I want. Is he there? He supplied this telephone number as his contact number. It is about the baby...'

'About the baby, you say?' A female voice offers to take a message for mister Florn. The female, she sounds quite young, possesses a characteristic accent. Hibernian?

'It is important I speak with mister Florn *direct*. Can you get him to the phone?'

'I'm with him,' says the girl.

'Erm? *Good*. In that case, since you're with him, bring him to the phone, please.'

'What? When I told you I am with him I didn't mean *physically*. I meant I'm with him... as in we are *together*.'

'What does that mean?'

'I am with him, er, you know, in respect of the fact I am seeing him. We are looking after the wee one *together*. At his place. Do you understand? I am living with George. I am staying in his bedroom. Do you get what I'm saying?'

'You live with him? Oh! I see. You are sharing child-keeping duties and so forth, with your mister Florn? Is that what you mean?'

'If you like.'

'Good. In that case, I wonder if you might help. I'm sure you know that George has linked-up the baby with a woman we have here at our centre who reported a baby *missing*. Through diligent and, I do not mind saying so, meticulous detective work, your George pieced together a rather extraordinary jigsaw. But, you see, we need to positively fix the identity of the child before we can reunite her with the probable mother. So I need mister Florn to bring the infant here so we might conduct DNA and blood tests. Once we are satisfied, we can reunite the baby.'

'Here?'

'To our Harmondsworth site. Home Office immigration, West London.'

'If the test is conclusive, would I leave the baby with the mother?'

'Of course! She'll be reconciled. They'll be reconciled. Mother and child.'

'How long will tests take? How swiftly will we get results?'

'I'd aim to have the tests completed overnight.'

'So we would stay in London overnight until they get the results confirmed?'

'Yes, I am afraid so. Could you manage that?'

'I don't see why not. I'll ask George for more cash. And I'll come over with the babby.'

'And regarding mister Florn? What about him? Will the gentleman be with you?'

'Does he *need* to be?'

'I don't suppose he does, it's not *essential*. But we would like to thank him for his detective work and logical thinking in such a complex case.'

'I don't think he'll be able to attend. You see? He's somewhat, *erm*, he's somewhat *otherwise* engaged. I will pass on your kind messages...'

'That's fine. What is your name? When do you think you will be able to bring the baby to us?'

'My name is Eimear. Eimear Lambe, spelled L-A-M-B-E. I can bring the baby right now!'

'Shall we say tomorrow?' Will you be using this phone number?'

'Yes, this is my phone. Tomorrow will be great! Can I take a refer-

ence number? Only, I have learnt over the last few weeks that if I
don't take a case reference number, the officials often mislay my
file...'

'Oh? Yes, zero zero zero one three six zero zero zero two eight zero
zero zero point zero zero zero four.'

'Um, thanks. *I think.* And you are?'

'As I said, my name is Bockett. Owen Bockett.'

'Ok, so.'

'See you tomorrow.'

'Time?'

'Lunchtime will suit.'

15

Eimear pays sixty pounds cash for an Aer Lingus to Dublin. The lady at the counter says, "Coming back?" Eimear shakes her head. Eimear hands over two fifty notes which, of course, have to be checked by a supervisor to verify legitimacy. Everyone in England knows the Irish cannot be trusted. A snotty-looking manager is called. She runs an ultraviolet light across the banknotes. She glares into Eimear's face, doubtless checking upon her credibility. After careful consideration, the go-ahead is given. The air-ticket is printed. The change, issued in Euros, is authorised.

Eimear finds a grey-brown polyvinyl chair to flop into. She pushes against the back-rest. At that precise moment, her phone vibrates. 'George? Is that you?'

"Yellow. It's me. How are you doing, young miss?"

'I'm fine, George. I'm in the airport. I have a flight. I have a flight *back home.*'

There is a pause before George speaks again: 'Ow did it go? Did the checks on the young un' come through fine?'

'Yes, they made them overnight like they said they would. And the DNA matched. You are so smart, George. I don't know how you did it. Nobody knows how you did it! The head guy here, a fellah named

Sprocket, I think, anyway, he was disappointed you couldn't make it. I didn't tell him why you could not come, of course. But he wanted to thank you *personally*. He said you were a hero. This fellah, mister *Sprocket*, asked me to pass on the thanks of his whole team. Though, from what I could see, his whole team comprised of just *him*.'

'And what's the little one's mum like?'

'Amira's mum? She is adorable. She is younger than I expected. She doesn't speak English.'

'I'm *glad* I wasn't there to see her take 'er baby back.'

'Glad? Why would you say that, George? After all this time I *still* do not understand you. You have a peculiar way of looking at things.'

There was another long pause. 'The police telephoned me at home.'

'They did? What did they want? Another interview?'

'They said insufficient evidence to prosecute.'

'What does that mean?'

'They said I don't have to go back to the station. In Eff Aye.'

In Eff Aye? What does that mean?'

There is another long interlude while the old man chooses his next words. 'They said they would send a letter to confirm. They said that's it.'

'That's what?'

'It.'

'Hey? Have you heard from Nigel?'

'Yeah. He and Arnie have brook up. That's the end of their relationship. He is in terrible shape. I said he should stay *with me* for a while. Until we get over things. He's real cut up about losing 'er. But maybe it's for y'best... Anyway, I said he ought to stay with me.'

'That's a splendid idea, George.'

'I said he should get another dog *too*. He was sad about getting rid of his dog...'

'Yes, I know he was.'

'Anyway, young miss, I don't wanna 'old yer up.'

'George, before you go... I know you said I should keep the money.

But it is a lot of cash. I didn't think it through before. But now I have. And I think maybe I should return it?'

'I want you to have *all* of it, Miss Yemarr. That is my genuine wish. I would like you to *start over*. I'd be glad if you did something good with that oodle. That is what I'd *really* like. *Please* keep it.'

'What would Nigel say? What would Nigel think?'

'It's not his cash. It's mine. And it's not up to him what I do with my war-chest. But I can't talk about it anymore because I don't know how much balance is left on this phone.'

'Do you know I will never see you again, George? Do you know that?'

'We're splashing in the tide, you and me, miss. That is all we are doing. Just splashing in the tide.'

'Aye. Until the next wave, then.'

'Bye.'

AUTHOR'S NOTES

Every year, more than 12,000 refugees arrive on the British coast after crossing the dangerous waters of the English Channel. The Channel migrants often use inadequate and overloaded boats.

In a single day, in August 2021, 800 migrants crossed the Channel. Most made the trip by inflatable dinghy. In 2021 at least forty-four people died or went missing on the perilous crossing.

Most of those who arrive on British shores come from Yemen, Eritrea, Chad, Egypt, Sudan, Iraq, and Syria. Official figures show that these asylum seekers are granted refugee status on their first hearing. Among the top five nationalities arriving by boat, 60% are routinely accepted as refugees, following an initial assessment. Figures obtained by the Refugee Council suggest that only a third of those arriving on British beaches are *not* officially considered to be refugees.

In 2020, two children, aged six and nine, were among four people who disappeared when their boat sank off the coast of France. Afterwards, an inspection of a detention facility at the Port of Dover revealed that at least 320 children arrived that summer. We might suppose that about 10% of *all those* who crossed the English Channel from June to August 2020 were children, though the UK government has *never* published exact figures for child migrant crossings.

In June 2021, The Daily Mail newspaper reported that a "baby in arms" and four "toddlers" were among 158 migrants who crossed the Channel in four small boats. A typical comment from the public (Evening Standard, September 2021) is that these migrants and refugees are "parasites" who bring "diseases" and "breed like rats" to "claim all the benefits."

For years, the UK government has worked on ideas that might deter these desperate people, portrayed as a *"tide of immigrants"* by right-leaning commentators. Such immigrants are deemed "illegal" because they enter the UK without authorization and do not have the required documentation. What can be done?

There are now more than twelve million people over the age of sixty-five in the UK. That is about a fifth of the entire adult population.

People with spectrum disorders such as Asperger's syndrome might be highly intelligent, but they do not communicate well with others. They often become preoccupied with *niche* topics and can become *obsessively* interested in a hobby. A pejorative term for this type of person is 'geek.' It is commonly accepted that *geeks* have an abnormal appreciation for numbers, patterns, routines, and charts.

In Britain, the slang term for such a person is 'anorak.' The British Medical Association estimates that around 700,000 people in the UK might be diagnosed with an autism spectrum disorder.

ALSO BY

Slutting The Globe
  by Neil Mach

Not only a humorous sexscapade, Slutting The Globe is *also* a full discourse on female empowerment!

A woman directs her life. She regains sensuality. She earns sovereignty. She hunts men. She grabs them with both fists. She frees herself from male guardianship. Here is a woman who enjoys using *erotic capital*.

Slutting The Globe is also about the *incompetence* of most guys. They are *not* roosters. They are pussy-cats!

If you are searching for a sex manual, this might be the best place to start! Because it's not a voyeuristic study of bosoms, nozzles, and gaping notches, it is a book about the *whys* of carnal experience, not the *hows*. You will enjoy watching a queen-bee sprout her wings, spread her legs, and conquer the world of useless men. Get It Now!

ABOUT THE AUTHOR

Neil Mach was born and raised in Surrey.

A rock 'n' roll kid he works as a music journalist, an editor, a podcast show-host, and a full-time author. He lives with his wife Sue in their small bungalow on the riverbank at Staines.

Neil has two daughters, Tanna and Perdie

I'd like to dedicate this book to the memory of my grandfather-in-law, Edgar George 'Pop' Doward of Putney. The original (and best) Patternmaker!

AUTHOR LINKS

Author Links

http://www.neilmach.me/author

https://twitter.com/neilmach

http://www.neilmach.me/author

Printed in Great Britain
by Amazon

31634995R00109